I0683752

When Water Becomes Thicker Than Blood

Sherrad O'Neil Glosson

Copyright © 2011 Sherrad O'Neil Glosson

All rights reserved.

ISBN-13: 978-0-578-09409-0

Editor Dr. Frances Curtis-Fields

Co-editor & Typesetting Mrs. Angelique Glosson-Spires

Book cover design by Savy Design

ACKNOWLEDGMENTS

Thank God for given me a mind to be creative. Without the gift of creativity I don't believe my first book and publishing company Wholethang Publishing Co. would not have come into fruition.

Special thanks to my mom Mrs. Angelique Glosson-Spires and my step dad Mr. Darryl Spires for their continued support, love and encouragement. My daily calls to my mom encouraging me to not let my mistake hinder my future. We learn from our mistakes, but keep it moving forward.

Big hug to my grandparents Pastor Hezekiah Williams and Mother Josie Williams and the Tabernacle of Judah Church of God In Christ family, thanks for your many prayers.

Special thanks to both of my aunts Mickey and Shawn, my uncle Malik, cousins Britni, Jarrel, Tiffany , and Demetres. Supportive friends Terrence West -Teknekemusic (Seasac Publishing), Wayne Pittman—City Slickers Shoes, DeAndre , Tony, LaSalle , Deeyonna , Stephaney since middle school you have been a true friend, coming to visit me and showing much love, I appreciate you young Steph. My Canadian friends Heidi, Amanda, Amber, Tek, Aimurban McCaulay-King Group Inc., Ace Styles- Touch 4 Touch Entertainment Inc. My entire Glosson & Smith family. I cannot name everybody, but you know I appreciate you. My homeboys from upstate, half-dead, what's up man I found a new outlet, you will be out in a few more years hold on and be strong, trublu.

Special thanks to my lil cousin Ranji Shaw who reads 24-7 and the first person to read my manuscript. She gave me two thumbs up.

Special thanks to Mr. Anthony Roy Milligan, Jr. He is a young author from Pontiac, Michigan.

SPECIAL THANKS

So now that I got all of that out of the way, it's time to give a special shout out to all of my haters, naysayers, and all the people who thought this was not going to come to realization. I could not have done this without you especially. Special love goes out to all of the people who I hung with in the streets everyday that still have not wrote or contacted me since I have been locked up. I'm not mad, they told me when I first came down what was going to happen.

DEDICATION--Shouts out to all my people who are locked up with me, who have being doing this prison bid just as I have day in and day out. Just because we are in prison doesn't mean that we have to be imprisoned. It trips me out sometimes when I think about when I was writing on pieces of kite paper, then a year later it turned into this, much love and see you on the yard.

Last but surely not the least, shout out to my lil cuz Shania Jonae. When I left when she was only 7 yrs old. She has encouraged me on several phone conversations and she still remembers me. See you soon.

CHAPTER 1

It's 12:19 a.m. and I just got off work from the Michigan State Fair on Eight Mile and Woodward. It was crazy today. My first day on the job and I had to deal with a million Mickey Mouse looking kids with face paint everywhere. I'm tired as hell and I can't wait to get home and get some sleep. I know my girl Maria gon' try and rape a nigga as soon as I step in the door, but she just gon' have to charge them batteries up and get it on her own.

I walked down Woodward to the Seven Mile bus stop and it seems like I been standing there forever waiting on the bus.

"Who the hell is this keep circling the block in this green Neon?" I say to myself pulling on my Black and Mild Cigar leaning against the bus stop sign. I inhaled, exhale, and suck the smoke back in through my nostrils. I already seen this car come around twice and at this point, I'm starting to get noided. Living in Detroit you can never be safe at a bus stop this time of night. Good thing I don't have my Cartier's on, otherwise I would be an easy target.

I pulled on the tip of the cigar again, and exhaled, sucking the smoke through my nose. It's damn near 12:30 and I've been standing here for a while waiting on this slow as D.O.T. Who da hell could they be looking for around here this time of night? They gotta be lost or something. "Damn!" It looks like they coming back around now.

The green Neon stopped right in front of me and rolled down the passenger window. It was a white woman who looked like she had to be in her forties. She don't look that bad either, but what the hell is she doing? I know this can't be a prostitute riding around looking for dick instead of walking. I guess that's the definition of motel on wheels.

"Hey Jimmy!" she shouted out the passenger window.

I pulled on the lit Black and Mild and acted like I didn't even hear her, although I was the only one at the bus stop. She couldn't have been talking to me, cause my name ain't no damn Jimmy.

"Hey Jimmy, I got that for you!" she shouted again.

She gotta be a drunk thinking she in West Bloomfield or some damn where in the burbs, cause if I was any other Detroiter, she probably would have been robbed by now.

I looked toward East Seven Mile then I looked west. I gave her eye contact and she waved me to come closer to the car. I pointed to the center of my chest, and she nodded her head. I walked up to the passenger window and looked in. She opened the door.

"Get in silly!" she said.

I looked around seeing if anybody noticed this but there was nobody in sight. I stepped one foot in the car, then the other, and as soon as I shut the door. ZOOM! The Seven Mile bus came flying past outta nowhere.

The whole car smelled like she had smoked a whole pack of cigarettes. I looked in the ash tray and it was about twenty cigarette butts in it with red paint at the end of the filter. I just sat there looking straight ahead as she took off down West Seven Mile. I lived this way anyway so it's a joy ride to me.

"It's under the seat!" she said.

In my mind I'm thinking, "What the hell is she talking about?" I'm confused, but I still wanted to see what "it" was, so I reached under the seat, but couldn't feel anything.

"Did you find it?" she asked.

I stretched my arm under the seat a little more, almost damn near to my elbow, and felt something hard like steel. I figured it had to be what she was talking about, so I pulled it from under. As I pulled it out, it had a little weight to it and by that time I realized what it was. It was a Mustard Green .357 without the hammer in the back of it.

"What is this?" I asked her with a puzzled look on my face.

"It's yours silly!" she started laughing. "The other thing is in the console, open it up!"

In my mind all I can think about was this exclusive ass gun I just came across, all because some dumb ass white woman thinks my name is Jimmy. I know I can sell this in the hood for at least a 'G' easy. I use to sell guns to drug dealers faithfully, like gas stations sold loosies when I was a youngsta, and if I came through with something like this... "CHA-CHING!" What else could she possibly have for me, or better yet, "Jimmy," whoever this nigga is?

I opened the console, and its a manila envelope. I pulled it out, took off the rubber band that it had on it, opened it up, and it was MONEY! One, two, three, foe, fi, si, se, eight, hundred dollar bills, CRISPY at that! My immediate thought was, "I just hit a lick that nobody would believe, and I'm about to jump outta this car as soon as she stop."

We approached a yellow light about to turn red at Seven Mile and Lasher. I'm looking around to make sure ain't no police around cause I'm about to dash and haul my ass outta here. I looked at her and she bobbing her head to what sounds like some damn Kid Rock. I turned my head back to the window, thinkin' I had to move quick cause the light is bout to turn green in about ten seconds. I reached for the door handle about to make my move.

"I got everything else back at the motel, that's where I'm headed right now."

She had my undivided attention I drew my hand back because I already got a pistol and some money. I knew whatever she has at the room gotta be even betta. The light turned green and she pulled off still bobbing her head and humming.

She made a left on Telegraph Road and drove down to the Econo Lounge. She pulled into the parking lot and parked the car. I sat still while she got out and opened the door. I still think she's a prostitute cause she got on some blue jean shorts that look like they were pants that she cut up. The white stockings with holes and runs in them, and the red heels with one heel broken, had prostitute written all over her body. Oh, not to mention the heavy red lipstick.

The door was open and I could see the whole room from the car, and it looked pretty clean from where I was sitting. I figured it was safe so I opened the door and put one foot on the ground. I looked around one last time before stepping all the way out, and then I shut the door behind me. I put the pistol in my waist and the money in my back pocket. I brushed my face with my right hand and then proceeded to the door.

When I walked in, she was in the mirror putting her hair in a ponytail smoking a Salem cigarette. There were two beds and I sat on the one farthest from the door.

"Why are you so damn quiet Jimmy? GOSH!" She turned to me and asked with the Salem still in her mouth, with her eyes low, tryna keep the smoke from burning them.

"I'm just tired from work that's all. Do you mind if I go take a shower? I gotta get some of this dirt from off me."

"No, not at all, Silly. You know, you acting real strange, Jimmy."

I laughed at her remark and went into the bathroom.

"Damn, this lady crazy as hell! Why da hell she think my name Jimmy?" I thought to myself.

I left the door wide open as I jumped in the shower. I kept the pistol in my hand and I could see her sitting on the bed through the bathroom mirror. She lit up another cigarette and I quickly took a lil' five minute shower. Moments later, I got out and dried myself off and walked in the bedroom. She took her clothes off, and only her bra and panties were left on. She must be a big fan of the Michigan Wolverines or it was just a coincidence that her bra was gold and her panties were blue.

"Hey, look under the mattress!" She pointed to the bed where I was sitting.

I walked over and lifted up the mattress. It was another envelope under it, just like the one in the car. I pulled it out and looked in it; it was mo' money, twelve hundred CRISPY dollar bills. I started smiling because I know I don' came across a good thang, being this Jimmy.

"You do coke?" she asked me.

In my mind I'm thinking that she should know everything I do, being as though she thinks I'm somebody else. Ima play this game with her though and see what else I can get.

"You know I do coke, why would you ask me that?"

"Just making sure, cause you acting a little off tonight."

She reached under the bed she was sitting on and pulled out a Nike shoe box full of dope, and sat it on the bed. She made two lines wit some cardboard and snorted it like a pro.

"Damn! I guess it's my turn huh?" I asked.

She nodded her head. I don' hit a lick anyway so I guess a line won't hurt me. Although I never done coke before in my life, it couldn't be that bad. I sat down on the bed with the cardboard box in between us and started snorting. Midway through, I started immediately sneezing, like six times back to back. It was like I had pepper taped to the bottom of my nose. My eyes were watery and I could tell by then that this had to be the purest coke in all of North America. Either that or the natural affects for a first timer.

By the time I finished the rest I heard a loud noise. "Is that a train?" I said to myself. The tripped out part about it was that the train was in my head and bells was ringing loudly. "What the hell did I just get myself into, or better yet, who is Jimmy?" I thought.

I fell back onto the bed with my hands stretched out like I had been shot in the chest and I couldn't move for shit, feeling like I was stuck under the train by that point.

"Do you want some liquor?" She asked me.

Speechless, all I could do was nod my head and stare at the ceiling. I couldn't even speak to say, No Thank you.

"Do you?" she asked again.

I thought I had nodded my head the first time but I nodded it again.

"I'll just get you some anyway."

Apparently, I thought I was moving my head, but the coke got me so fucked up; my body here, but my mind is on the other side of town.

"I gotta get some ice. I'll be right back."

She walked outta the room and slammed the door. It seemed like as soon as she did that, I snapped back into reality from being hypnotized. I jumped up and began to make my move from the motel. I scrapped the left over dope that was left on the cardboard back into the box and wiped the residue that was on the right side of my pinky finger onto my pants. I put the gun in my waist and made sure I had the money. Noided, I thought I heard something outside. I started making my way to the door so I could get the hell outta sight A.S.A.P.; already knowing which way I was going to run once I opened the door. I heard a knock, my eyes got big and I stopped moving I didn't even want to breathe. I just looked at the door, took a deep breath, and swallowed.

"Jimmy, it's me. I left the key on the table."

I looked on the table and behold, the damn key was sitting next to the 19" T.V. on the right side.

I slowly walked to the door, but I hesitated before opening it; again, I swallowed. I reached for the knob and then I swallowed again. I turned it slowly. She rushed through the door and she wasn't alone.

"POLICE, GET ON THE GODDAMN FLOOR!"

About eight cops came running behind her.

"It's him, he did it!" The woman shouted.

"WAIT! Did what? What the hell is going on?" I yelled throwing my hands in the air.

Coke went everywhere like I was squeezing a gigantic bottle of baby powder.

"Jimmy Porter, get on the GOD DAMN ground with your hands on your head!" The police yelled with their guns drew towards my head.

She screamed "He's in there, he's in the closet… he put him in the closet!"

"I did what? Who…?"

The policeman looked at me listening to what the blonde just said and slowly walked to the closet. He opened the door slowly and everybody in the room was looking to see what was getting ready to be revealed.

"HOLY!" The cop yelled.

It was a dead white man sitting on the floor, slumped over, with a bullet in his head.

"WHAT DA…?" was all I could say with my mouth wide open.

"Wait! Officer let me explain. My name is Leon Cook, I...I…"

"BAM!"

One of the officers slapped me across the back of the head with his gun. He then searched my body and found the .357 I had in my waist and pulled it out.

"Well, well, well, what do we have here?" He said holding the gun in the air like it was a toy, looking at one of his partners.

He checked the revolver and a bullet was missing.

"It looks like we don't have to do much work after all boys, looks like we got our number one suspect right here in front of our eyes, no need for the First 48 crew," he said.

All I could think about is my fingerprints all over the gun, the twenty stacks in the envelope, the dope, and this white man in the closet dead as a door knob.

I could hear a phone ringing but it seems like it was far, far, away. I was the only one hearing it I guess cause nobody responded. It sounds like it's right inside my ears. Damn that coke got me fucked up.

"RING…. RING…. RING…."

"Hel...hell...hello…"

"L.C., wake up man it's me! Man you won't believe what just happened to me Dawg!"

My mind was still going crazy over this long crazy ass dream I just had. It felt so damn real. I gotta stop drinking and smoking so much weed. Staggering outta the bed trying to hear what my homeboy, Tek, was yelling on the other end of the receiver.

"What's going on man?"

"Man some fool I got into it with at the club a while ago just tried to do me in!"

"What...? Who...?"

It's 6:17 a.m. in the morning and I can barely keep my eyes open, and Tek is telling me he just got shot at.

"HELLO!" he yelled.

"I'm h...hear man!"

"DAWG! Wake the hell up I need you to come get me from the McDonalds on Six Mile and Greenfield before he thinks he needs to circle back and finish me off!"

"You strapped up ain't you?"

"Man its six o'clock in the morning. All I wanted was a steak, egg and cheese bagel, extra seasoning and a large orange juice. Who would have thought that I was going to look death in the face this early? Hell, I ain't even hit my girl yet."

"A'ight man, I'm on my way."

"Make it fast man!"

"A'ight!"

"Hurry!"

"A'ight nigga!" I yelled hanging up the phone.

I ran downstairs in the basement, went to my stash and grabbed a .45. I ran back upstairs and threw on the clothes I had on the night before. I looked at my girl, Maria, and she was still sleeping heavily so I grabbed the keys and hopped in my ride to go pick up Tek.

Tek and I met when I was in prison doing a two year bid for pistol charges a lil' while ago. He was on a four year bid, but he had already done two by the time we became bunkies, for armed robbery. One day we were on the basketball court playing two on two; me and Tek against some cats that just came in from a level four. One of the guys kept trying to get buck with me every time I came to the hole. Tek let it be known… "If any of you niggas foul my nigga that hard again, it's going to be a problem!" The game resumed, and then moments later I came through the lane again, the same guy clothes lined me across my face and my lip swelled up instantly. It was physical basketball to me, and I was cool, but Tek looked into the guy eyes and then walked off the court. At about 8:45, fifteen minutes before the yard was about to close, Tek caught him slippin' on the back forty and stabbed dude in the neck twice. I noticed police coming from everywhere, running to the back and when I looked at Tek, he was sweating bullets; nodding his head, to let me know he was the reason behind that. From that day forward, I showed my loyalty to Tek and he continued to show it to me.

When I pulled into the parking lot, Tek was nowhere to be found. I drove to the other side of the lot and spotted his red Caprice on twenty-eight inch rims, it had bout twelve bullet holes in the driver side. "Where da hell dis nigga at?" I wondered. I called his cell phone looking around the parking lot hoping to see him jump outta somewhere. He picked up.

"Nigga, you here yet?"

"Yeah fool, where you at?"

He had his front seat laid all the way back, duckin down wit his hat low, and popped his head up like a damn turtle outta his shell.

"Man! What the hell took you so god damn long?"

"I was sleep, you know that right? Man look at yo ride tho'!" I said laughing.

"Oh, you think it's funny?"

"You ain't get shot did you? Therefore, HELL YEAH it's funny!"

I could tell he was pissed about his ride. I could see it in his eyes that he wanted revenge.

"You on the phone talkin' bout, L.C., hurry man, come get me, he might come back. Sounding like a damn fairy; over here scared, duckin down and shit!"

"Man, FUCK YOU!" We busted out laughing. "Take me to the crib so I can change real quick!"

"A'ight, hold on. I'm hungry now; let me get something to eat. You still want that bagel you was feenin' for?"

"Hell naw, but I do want my ride back."

"YEAH, well you gotta take that to T.O.L. on Mound now."

I got my food and left from McDonalds to take Tek to his crib.

"What happened any way between you and Dawg?" I asked.

"Man, let me tell you. I was in the club doing my one, two thang as usual and I noticed this lil' red bone tryin to get at me. You know me, I'm down for whatever. So I take her to the bar and we get a couple of drinks. I'm tryna get her all the way wide open now. All of a sudden this Cuba Gooding Jr., from Boyz in The Hood look-alike, was tryin to get buck wit me. He yelling, throwing drinks all on the floor, making a scene. One of them I gotta fight every night just to prove my love ass nigga. I sat there for a minute, remaining humble as always, but this fool kept talking. Man I lost it, I hit him so hard in his left ear and knocked him right out. He didn't even see it coming!"

"Straight up!" I said laughing.

"Man look, dat boy's ear swoll up like Mr. Potato Head."

It was too funny listening to Tek talk about what happened that night. He always made a joke outta a story. It's never a dull moment when Tek opens his mouth, but there's one thing I know fosho, in a city like Detroit, it's always retaliation. Even on the smallest things, you can get gunned down for just looking at somebody for two seconds long.

CHAPTER 2

After I dropped Tek off I went back home and Maria was still sleeping. I walked in and kissed her on her forehead.

"Hmmm, hey Papi!" she yarned.

"Hey baby, how you feeling?"

"I was just about to get up and cook you breakfast."

Maria was with me before I went to prison for two years. She stuck by my side through the whole bid, and held me down tough. She kept my house bills paid as well as my car notes. She even helped me get my barber, hair and nail salon jumped off when I got out. She's this peanut butter skin toned, five foot three, Dominican Republic, Spanish talking goddess. I met her downtown at the Fox Theater on

Woodward, across the street from Comerica Park, when I went to this play called "Diary of a Mad Black Woman" a play by the famous Tyler Perry.

I went alone and of course it was single women everywhere, which was my whole intention of going alone in the first place. As I was coming outta the theater, it was about four Spanish-looking females looking at the same brochures at the information desk; talking and giggling amongst each other.

I went over to them and stood next to this Pocahontas, and asked her what her name was in Spanish. I know I had caught her off guard but that was the point from the start.

"Con-permiso" she replied blushing like she didn't hear what I said he first time.

I grabbed her hand and placed a kiss on the back of it.

"mellamo Leon, yi tu"

"Me llamo Maria." She said putting her hand over her mouth like she was shy.

After that, we went off real good for a good week. I took her on dinner dates in Chicago, Florida and I even took her to Mexico. I showed a side of a man that most women don't see from a hood nigga coming out of Detroit, and she was so gon' like Monica. We were downtown coming out of the

Greektown Casino heading to the Pittsburg and the Seattle Sea Hawks Super bowl game, it was people everywhere on the sidewalk and streets, drinking, smoking, dancing, you know, having a good time. Some clown starting runnin' his mouth cause' he couldn't hold his liquor, and I had to up the burner on him just to shut him up. I mean, it wasn't like I was gon' shoot him. I just wanted to show him that what he was saying could easily be put on hold just by the thought that he could be shot. Niggas from Detroit is known for acting a fool when something is going on downtown, and true enough, he was one of the few reasons why tourist don't come to the MURDA' MITTIN' as some would call it. You'll be surprised at how a gun can make a grown man piss on himself when he sees the tip of it facing his way. It just so happened, I was slippin', and it was an undercover cop standing across the street watching the whole thing. He arrested me and took me to 1300 Beaubian. They could have charged me with felonies assault, but my lawyer got me a two flat for the gun. Maria stayed by me the whole bid and I didn't even get a chance to put my meat game down.

I jumped in the shower and moments later I smelled bacon coming through the vents. "Damn that smells good," I said to myself.

I heard her cell phone ring and when she answered it, she was quiet. All of a sudden she started yelling at whoever was on the other end. I thought nothing of it at first and just kept taking my shower. About five minutes later, I got out and by that time Maria had piped down. I wrapped my towel around my waist and went to open the door. WHAM! A frying pan came swinging at me. I slammed the door back quickly.

"Maria! What the hell are you doing, girl?" I yelled.

"Leon, I don' told you about messing around on me!"

"What?"

"Ima put a end to this right now!" She hit the door with the pan again.

"What are you talking about?"

"Who the hell was at the club with you last weekend, Leon?"

I know she pissed off because she called me Leon instead of Papi. "What are you talking about?"

"You know exactly what I'm talking about, don't play dumb, boy. My sister said she saw you leave with one of them dancer hoes from All Stars at five in the morning!"

DAMN! I forgot her sister works there. She caught me slippin good this time.

"UH...I don't know what you talking about baby, I...."

"Don't baby me dammit!" Her black side was starting to come out. It got quiet seconds later and I start turning the door knob slowly hoping that she wouldn't be still standing there waiting for my head to pop out. I peeked my head out to see if the coast was clear.

"SPLASH!"

She threw a glass vase at the door as I immediately shut it back.

"I hate you, you sorry son of a....!" She screamed with a raging voice. "You gotta come out the bathroom someday, Leon. You know what? I'm outta here."

I rushed out the bathroom before she could grab anything else and tackled her onto the couch. I sat on top of her naked with her on her back and her hands pinned above her head. Tears were coming down her cheeks.

"Listen to me, Maria. I wasn't at the club with nobody. You hear me?" I tried to plead my case.

"Leon, get... the... hell... off me!" she said tryna use her little strength to get loose.

She kneed me in the nuts and I rolled off the couch onto the floor and she ran out the door. I got up, wrapped the towel around my waist, and ran right behind her.

When I got outside she had a baseball bat in her hand standing next to my brand new Mustang. My heart damn near dropped straight to my feet.

"MARIA, WAIT..!" I shouted.

She took the titanium steel slugger and swung it like she was Barry Bonds on steroids for real, at my windshield. By that time, my heart was on my toes.

"BITCH! What the hell you doing?" I yelled with my hands on my head and my mouth wide open in shock.

"BITCH? Oh I got yo bitch!" she said walking around to the back end of the car smashing out a tail light.

"Dammit, Maria, can we please talk about this?"

I fell to my knees, surrendering so she could stop abusing my precious baby.

"There ain't shit to talk about, Leon!" she said still holding the bat in her hand looking at the car.

"I'm sorry Bay...." I pleaded.

"Yeah, you sorry alright, you da sorriest man I ever met in my life. How could you Leon? After all I done did for you. This is how you repay me?"

I remained speechless on my knees as she poured out her heart to me.

We got into it often, but this time she took it on a whole different level. She walked to her car without even looking back at me and she sped off listening to "I'm Bossy" a song by Kellis.

I stood there looking at my car in amazement. I got insurance so it really don't matter, however, it still don't scratch the fact that I just bought it like three weeks ago.

"Damn, I gotta run to my shop". I ran into the house and threw my clothes on.

Moments later I came out, hopped on my bike, and headed to my shop downtown.

Sherrad O'Neil Glosson

CHAPTER 3

It's a beautiful day outside. The weather feels like it's about 90 degrees. Not a single cloud in the air and its ballas, and ballets everywhere around downtown. I'm cruzin' down Jefferson slowly watching crowds of people go in and out of Hart Plaza. It's a Techno Fest or something going on. Whatever it is, it's pumped over there. It couldn't have been a better day for me to ride my bike, and I hardly remember that my car is smashed up. I pull right up to the door of my shop and walk in. My auntie immediately gives me eye contact, and I already know why.

"How you gon' tell us to be at work on time and you show up an hour late?"

I busted out laughing cause I knew this was coming.

My auntie is the manager of my shop, and I have her taking care of things when I'm out and about. She's been doing hair since before I was born, and she's like a Guru when it comes to braiding.

She made braids more popular when she started puttin' these wicked designs in this famous NBA Star's head. Every since then, braids have become a well known common hair style, especially for black men. She used to do hair out of her basement, but figured she'll help me jump my business off with her expertise.

"I had to deal with a light situation with Maria this morning." I replied.

"Again?" she asked.

"It's a long, long, story, Auntie. I really don't feel like talking about it."

"Boy, I don' told you about messing with them foreign women. You betta quit playin with they emotions before they catch you while you sleeping and cut yo you-know-what off!" She motioned her hands in a cutting motion.

"Snip, Snip!!" One of the other employees added.

"You'll wake up hollering like Kunta Kinte' in Roots!" my auntie joked. Then, the whole shop burst out into laughter, including me.

My auntie always has a joke to dish out. I set myself up for that one. In a way, I was a little embarrassed; I just went into my office to look at the mail. I sat down behind the desk and put my head back brushing my face with both hands.

"L.C., what's up?" My concentration was broken.

"Hey, Tony how you doin', man?"

"Aw, man, L.C. I'm doing real good man, and I know you told me to stop saying this but I just-"

"Tony…" I cut him off, "I know you appreciate me giving you a chance."

"Yeah, but L.C. I just wanna-"

"Tony! I told you man, you welcome!"

Tony is this young Hispanic kid from the neighborhood. He's only seventeen years old, and has been in and outta jail his whole childhood. His mom is a crack head and his father is doing life in Cali for a triple murder. He learned how to cut hair behind bars, and when he came to my shop, and told me his story, I had to give him a chance. Since then, he's been on a right path. Every time he needs somebody to talk to, I'm right there for him. He keeps trying to thank me for giving him an opportunity every time I see him.

My cell phone rang and broke up the frivolous conversation that we always have, and I stepped outside the building to take the call.

"What's up, Lo?"

Lo is my 2nd cousin. We don't really hang out that much, but when we do, we act a monkey!

"What up, Cuz? What's hood?"

"Nothing much man just down here at the shop checking up on things. You know how I do! What's hood wit you?"

"You feel like hitting up Kingdom tonight?"

"The Kingdom, uhh….. Yeah we can do that. I'll be there later on tonight I gotta take care of some other things before then, but I'll be there."

"A'ight cool, just call me when you're on your way."

We hung up the phone, and I was about to call up Tek to see what he had planned for tonight, but I remembered; he and my cousin don't get along too well. I put my phone in my pocket and turned to go back in the shop. I noticed this Caucasian woman walking down Jefferson on the other side of the street. She looked like she was about five four. She had blonde hair and with more curves than Stacey Dash. She had to be mixed with something cause you hardly ever see a white woman strapped from head to toe like this one. I guess it's part of the new phenomenon. Technology is changing, so I suppose the human physique is also.

I stood there rubbing my hands together trying to figure out how I was going to make my move because too many cars were coming down Jefferson, since it was something going down at Hart Plaza. I had to catch up with this woman quick before she got outta my eye sight. I looked around and just my luck, an old white man, who had to be in his eighties, was standing alongside the curb trying to get across the street as well. He had a silver pole in his hand that had a red tip at the end of it. He had the biggest shades I had ever seen in my life on his face. I walked up to him and tapped him on his shoulder.

"Excuse me, Sir." I said.

He turned around with the pole and hit me in the leg with it.

"Oh, I'm sorry about that." he said. Suddenly, it made sense. He was blind.

"Are you trying to get to the other side?" I asked.

"Well, yes Sir, I am."

"I think the lights are broken, I'll walk you across."

"Okay, young man."

He grabbed my arm and as soon as we stepped onto Jefferson the cars started slowing down. As we were making our way to the other side, the woman I was trying to pursue was watching so that made my chances even better. I smiled as I walked him across the street realizing that my plan couldn't have been executed any better. I should be on one of those Mentos (the fresh maker) commercials.

"Thank you, young man!" he replied once we met our destination.

"No problem sir, thank you!" I responded, cause he just don't know how he just helped me out. We both came out on the winner's side. He went on about his way, and now it was time for me to make my move.

"Excuse me Ms. Lady, my name is L.C." I put my hand out for her to shake it.

"I'm Becky!" she gave me her right hand and I kissed the back of it.

"Oh, so you're a gentleman all the way across the board, huh?" She asked with a soft voice.

"Well I try to be, Ms. Becky!" I burst out into laughter.

"What's that for?"

"Oh, nothing!" all along I'm thinking about the lyric's from the rapper Plies called, "Gimme Dat Becky".

Standing there looking at this beautiful queen in front of me, with these blue stiletto heels, black jeans, and blue button down shirt showing off the matching belly button ring, and not to mention her eyes were as blue as the sky.

"So, where you headed?" I asked her, trying to be smooth.

"I'm looking for this nail salon my home girl told me about and I'm lost, I think."

She looked at the directions in her hand and then looked at the names of the buildings that were in front of us.

"Well, well, well, today is your lucky day cause I happen to own a barber, hair, and nail salon across the street!" I smiled, rubbing my chin.

"Is that right?" she was intrigued, I could tell.

"I'm sure it wouldn't be a problem with you getting in the booth A.S.A.P. either."

She looked at her directions once more and threw it on the ground.

"Okay, well lead the way, Mr. L.C.!"

She wrapped her arm around mine and we walked across the street. The whole time all I could think about was how my auntie was gon' eat this girl alive, especially once I say her name. I opened the door and Becky went in first. The whole shop stopped what they were doing and focused their whole attention on us.

"Everybody, this is Becky."

There was complete silence for about five seconds, and Becky just waved at everybody. Moments later, the whole shop burst out laughing, falling out the chairs, with tears coming down their faces.

"Is there something funny?" she asked.

"Girl, you never heard that song by Plies called "Becky"?" my auntie asked.

Becky went into deep thought and when she realized she was hip to it, she gave me a little shove to the side.

"Oh, so you think you funny, huh?" she remembered me doing the same laugh when she told me her name outside.

"Aw, come on, you gotta admit it was a little funny. It just caught me off guard!" I said smiling.

"Yeah okay, Mr. Funny Man!" she started smiling as well. She went to the nail booth and I followed her.

"So, Ms. Becky, do you know what I had to go through just to get to you?"

"Oh, so you thought that by using that blind man was going to work?" I nodded my head.

"It did I gotta give you that. You was real smooth!" she smiled.

"You have a pretty smile, you know that?"

"Thanks!" she replied.

"I see you don't have a ring on your finger. What, you haven't found that special someone yet?"

"Naw, not really, I don't have a man or any kids."

"Is that right?" BINGO! I thought to myself smiling.

"What you cheezin' for? You got some kids?" she said raising her left eyebrow

"Nawll, it's just a rare thing to find a women without any kids now a days, especially a woman of your caliber."

"A women of my caliber? and what caliber am I, Mr. L.C.?"

"I mean look at you, you look like you keep yourself together, and you seem intelligent thus far. It is hard for me to believe that nobody has swooped you up yet."

"Is it that they haven't swooped me, or I haven't swooped them up?" she smiled.

"Oh ok Ms. Independent that's what I am talking about. I think I am in need of some swooping".

She busted out laughin'.

We conversed the whole time she was getting her nails done and I could tell she was feeling me.

"Finished" the lady doing her nails said turning off the fan that was blowing her nails dry.

"Oh girl, you did a real good job ima' have to come back next week. You have a card or something?" Becky asked.

I didn't hesitate pulling one out my back pocket.

"You know what, you are too much", she said smiling.

"Hell, I rather be too Damn much than not much at all."

"Ok, Nephew spit dat", my auntie was hatin' on me.

Becky finished getting her nails done and I walked her back across the street to her car.

"Oh, so you riding good too, huh?" looking at her all white BMW.

"It gets me around you know." she replied.

"So Miss Becky, tell me, when you gon' let me take you out and romance you a little bit?"

"Uh...let me see...whenever you're not busy Mr. Business Man."

"Oh, I always find time for pleasure."

"Well, in that case, how about tomorrow?"

"Tomorrow it is!" I replied and she gave me her number.

I headed back to the shop and went back into my office. I realized that I had a text message; it was from my home girl, Bamby, she was texting me again.

Me and Bamby use to talk back in the day when we was in high school. She used to be a dancer at the Brass Key on Livernois, and now she a bartender at Déjà Vu over on Six Mile and Woodward. She about five seven, hundred fifty five pounds, with more curves than Outer Drive Road, with green eyes. We hit it off for a minute, but then just became close friends. I left the shop and headed her way. I figured she really wanted to see me, being as though she has been calling me like crazy. It's been a while since we have seen each other, so I guess a lil of my time wont hurt a bit. Besides, I can use a drink or two, and a lil dance just to get my mind off what Maria did this morning. She really got me buggin' out cause' she got keys to my crib still. You never know what that girl might be up to.

Sherrad O'Neil Glosson

CHAPTER 4

I headed over to the Vu to see what she wanted. I hadn't seen her in a while and she been calling me like crazy lately. I've been wondering what she wanted so I guess I'll give her a little of my time.

When I walked in, she was standing behind the bar as usual serving up some drinks for these older looking men with suits on. They had to be on their lunch break. They must've just wanted to look at some booty before it was time to go back. I walked over to the bar and sat at the end. She was talking to one of the guys she was serving. I just sat there looking at her ass. She was wearing some tight red spandex shorts. When she turned around and noticed me, she was in total bliss. I could tell by how she immediately started blushing from ear to ear.

"Hey baby, how you doing?" she said running towards me hugging me around my neck kissing me on the cheek.

"What's up, B? What's going on? I see you been calling me like crazy!"

"Where you been?"

"I've been taking care of some business, you know me."

"I haven't seen you in a while and I've been wanting to come by and chill with you."

"Is that right?" I wrapped my arms around her thin waist and pulled her close to me.

"Uh huh!" she nodded and sat on my lap.

I instantly became horny but I knew she was just tryna set things up for later. She started giving me a lap dance to a Ludacris song called "Sex Room". Slowly grinding on me, I was fully erect, and I almost gave in.

"Girl, what are you doing?" I asked.

"Trying to seduce you, is it working?"

"A lil!" I smiled. She grabbed my hard on and squeezed.

"You call that a little?" she said

"Where Big Ray at?" I changed the subject. "I didn't see him at the door when I came in."

"Yeah, he quit like a week ago. I think he works at a club downtown now."

"Dig that, why don't you go get me a drink?"

"What do you want?"

"Grey Goose on the rocks!"

"I'll be right back."

When she stood up I couldn't help noticing her fur burger poking out them shorts like a fist.

She left to go make my drink and I saw a guy in the back of the club, looking my way. It was hard to see his face cause it was dark. All I saw was his full grown beard. He had his hat real low though, and was mugging hard as hell. When he notice me looking at him he turned the other way.

Bamby came back with my drink and I took a sip.

"Oooh Wee…! That's how I like it!" I responded to the goose rushing down my throat into my veins.

"What time do you get off?"

"I think I get off at about ten or so, but until then Ima keep watching these fools get drunk and act a fool. They act like they haven't seen a naked woman since they came out the womb!" We started laughing.

"Girl, you silly!" I took another sip. "Aye, who is this clown in the back keep looking this way?" She looked in the direction I was referring to.

"I don't know, I never seen him before. He must've came in before you or right after you cause he wasn't here ten minutes ago."

I turned back around and took another sip of my drink and when I turned my head again, he was gone. "Who da hell was that?" I thought to myself.

"So when you gonna spend some time with me?" Bamby asked and I knew it was coming.

"Uh…?"

"See, that's what I be talking about right there!" She said rolling her eyes, shaking her head. I started laughing

"A'ight, A'ight, look…"

She folded her arms waiting to hear what I was about to say.

"Tomorrow I want you to call me and we gon' hook up and do our thing, A'ight?"

"Yeah whatever!" she said pouting, and I pulled her onto my lap.

"I'm serious, but now I gotta get me a dance before I leave, you know that's my song!"

Another song by Ludacris came on and I went and sat on the side of the stage with money in my hand. "How Low Can You Go…" is thumpin' through the speakers. Looking over at B, I could tell she was a little uneasy about this girl in front of me making her booty clap in my face. For some reason, she wanna get back wit a nigga. I mean Bamby is fine and all, but right now I'm cool on relationships. I started putting money in ole' girls G-String, looking over at Bamby through the corner on my eye. She still had her arms folded shaking her head.

After I got a couple shots of some Grey Goose in my system, and a few dances I left and headed to this shop over on Mound Rd. called Top of the Line Motoring. Top of the Line Motoring is one of the illist shops there is on the outskirts of Detroit.

When I walked in the building Sheela was sitting at the desk messing with her phone. Sheela and I met when I went to this community college in Flint, when I first graduated from high school. Her brother and I were roommates and played ball together for a year before I went over to Canada to play.

"Girl who you texting?"

"Hey what's up Leon, how you been?" she said standing up giving me a hug.

"I'm doing alright. I got a lil' problem".

"All hell, what happened?" she said looking out the door for my car.

"My ride is at home, I need ya'll to come pick it up for me sometime today."

"Keys", she put her hand up.

"Alrightie, thank you Sheela and tell your brother to hit me up a'ight'.

"Kay".

I left and went to my crib so I can change and hook up with Lo tonight. That Grey Goose had me kinda tipsy already. I might not need to drink tonight or at least not that much, but that is easier said than done. When Lo go out he is a drinking machine and I know for a fact that he gon' try and have me on lean all night long. He gets a real kick out of me when I am drunk.

I pulled up, and something seemed kinda strange. When I walked in the kitchen, the window was open; usually I double check all my windows before I leave the house. I guess after me and Maria got into it I was thrown off my square a lil' bit. Oh well, let me get in the shower and get ready. Gotta find me a replacement girl tonight.

CHAPTER 5

I called Top of The Line Motoring Shop where I took my car and they weren't done with it yet, so instead I rode my bike to Lo's house. I got there at about 9:30 p.m. or so and he was standing on the porch in a wife beater and some boxers.

"Man what da hell you doing?"

"What up cuz, somebody keeps playing with my doorbell. Ima catch who it is and Ima beat the living Jesus up out of them when I find out who they are. I know it's one of them little bay bay ass kids running around here loose as hell!" We started laughing.

"Remember when we use to do that?" I asked.

"Yeah, we always used to be getting our ass beat!" He replied. "Man, where is yo car at tho'?" Lo said, looking around like I was missing something.

"Man don't even ask, it's a looong... story".

"Yeah, Maria been drummin' you upside yo head again huh?"

I nodded in agreement then we went inside the house.

"Let me go change real quick I'll be back."

I sat on the couch and the news was on; they were talking about the state budget and how they were letting prisoners out early. Me and Lo did time before and it seemed like they said that every week but never did.

"A Lo you hear this?"

"What's that", he came in the front room half dressed.

"They talkin' bout' letting niggas out of the joint early."

"Yeah right, they were saying that shit when we were down, now of a sudden they tryna' let niggas go."

Lo had did time for an assault that he caught on a guy at the club over on Seven Mile one night. He got into it over some nonsense of course and smashed a bottle across his face knocking him out. Lo is notorious for buying niggas a drink and if you know like I know, you can damn near kill somebody with a Moet bottle.

"Let's ride out!" Lo said, coming back into the living room.

He had on his brown button up, blue jeans, with some brown Mauris. Look like they were the latest ones with the alligator tongue on'em and everything.

"Man where did you get them?"

"You know I had to stop by City Slickers." He was rubbing on them like they still alive or something.

"You see em'!" He replied trying to stunt."Did you see the eyes blink?"

"Man, get the hell outta here, you killin'em' I ain't gon' lie! Lets ride."

My outfit was similar but instead I had on a red Polo shirt with red Mauris. We hopped on our bikes and headed to the Kingdom Nightclub in downtown Detroit.

When we got there, it was people everywhere. The line was wrapped around the building. It had to be about an eight to one female to male ratio. The VIP line wasn't even half of the regular line so we went VIP.

"What's up Big Ray?"

"L.C., what's good, Baby?"

"I was at the Vu earlier looking for you."

"Yeah man, I just be bouncin' from club to club, you know?"

I met Big Ray when I was in the joint also. He use to always say when he got out he was going to be a security guard or a bouncer. He'll have seven hundred pounds on the flat bench talking about how he was going to be throwing people around like weight he was pushing. He was huge, about six seven, three hundred pounds of muscle. You thought Wesley Snipes was black, Big Ray was beyond black but he was my Homie. "Come on in, Dawg." he gestured.

When he opened the door Gucci Mane was subbing through the roof, "Rock star lifestyle might don't make it…"

"Damn Cuz, it's women everywhere!" Lo said excitedly.

"Hell yeah, we bout to get it in tonight, Baby. Let's hit the bar!" I was geeked by then we went to the bar and started off with a couple of shots of Patron and immediately we started feeling like we were blasted.

"Damn, man… I'm feeling it already!" Lo said bouncing to the words of Gucci Mane.

(song playing)…'Party, Party, Party, let's all get wasted, shake it for me baby girl. Do it butt naked…"

"What you gon' get to sip on cuz?" Lo asked me.

"Man just get me a Grey Goose and Cranberry."

"Grey Goose and Cranberry? Are you crazy? Naw, excuse me. Miss, can I get two bottles of Moet?" he told the bartender.

"Oh so you really tryna get me wasted huh?"

"Yeah fool why not? Let's get it in!"

"Man, you know how you be when you get a bottle of Moet in your hand."

"Man, I'm chillin' tonight. Lets have fun."

Like I haven't heard that before. I just shook my head.

"What? you don't believe me?" he asked as if he didn't know the answer to that.

We popped the bottles of Moet as soon as the bartender came back and started sipping right out the bottle. Either I was drunk already or thirsty cause I had Moet dripping down the side of my mouth when I turned the bottle up.

"Damn, Cuz is it a hole in yo mouth or is it just dat good?"

I busted out laughin', spitting it out cause I didn't know he was watching me the whole time.

"I'll be right back Dawg."

"Where you goin' fool?"

"I spilled some of this shit on my arm."

I headed to the bathroom and this female pulled me outta nowhere.

"Where you goin', Baby?"

"Umm…I'm heading to the restroom. What? You tryna come?"

She nodded her head yeah.

"A'ight look, let me go in first and wait about five minutes and then you come in, A'ight?"

She nodded her head and put the whole tip of her Corona bottle in her mouth.

"Damn baby it's like that huh?"

She licked her lips. She wasn't too bad looking either, but I was drunk anyway so at that time it was all good. I walked to the bathroom and as soon as I entered she was on my heels. I knew what she wanted to do so I went to the last stall and she followed me. The guy who was at the sink selling cologne, blacks and everything else didn't care and she didn't either. I pulled my pants down and got ready as she got on her knees and started serving me up like a pro.

Less than ten seconds after, I heard bangin' on the door.

"Aye, you gotta come outta there Homie!"

I know it ain't that hatin' ass sink boy. Ole' girl act like she didn't even hear him say a word. She had her legs sticking all out the door in the open. Dude on the other side of the door tapped her heels.

"Excuse me, Miss. You gotta come outta there!"

I pulled my pants up and left outta the bathroom smiling. I went back to the bar to meet up with cuz.

"Man what took you so long?"

"Man, I had a situation," we clung our bottles together and took a sip.

"Man, its mad hoes in here, im tellin' you, and I got these niggas heads in here turned looking down at my shoes."

"Would you like to dance?" A woman approached Lo and asked him while he was in motion to a sip.

"Hell yeah. Let's do it!"

As he headed to the dance floor, he turned around looking at me smiling. He was drunk as hell already. I had an excuse to be faded, but Lo on the other hand, had a low tolerance for alcohol. A shot of beer would have him bouncing off the walls.

After he left and headed to the dance floor, this five foot three, brown skin woman with long black hair that came down to the middle of her back, walked past me. I followed behind her.

"Excuse me, Miss. Would you like to dance?"

"Sure" she replied then led me to the dance floor.

I'm holding her hand with the bottle in my right and as she was walking in front of me.

"Baby, you looking real good tonight!" I said.

"Thank you!" she smiled.

By the time we got to the dance floor a song by Trey Songz called "Invented Sex" came on. It was the perfect song for the moment and I could tell how she was grinding on me that she was feeling the song also. I whispered lyrics from the song in her ear as we danced and she began to add a little more hip in her dip. (Song playing) 'Girl when I get you to the crib... up stairs to the bed... girl you gonna think, girl you gonna think, you gonna think I invented sex...

"What you doing later?" I asked.

"I don't know what you got in mind?"

"Well...we can go back to my crib and get to know each other a little better!"

"Hold on Big Boy, let's not jump the gun too fast now."

"I'm just saying. It'll be a lot easier for us to talk without all this music in our ears."

"Yeah you make a point there. Let me go tell my girls I'm leaving."

I went through the crowd looking for my cousin and didn't see him anywhere until I turned around and seen him standing in front of the stripper pole watching the girl who asked him to dance sliding down the pole up side down.

"A cuz, you see this shit?".

"Aw man, I'm bout to leave with this chick. You good for tonight?"

"Dawg, we just got here you tryna leave already?"

"Yeah fool I'm tryna get laid wit it, not look at it all night!"

"A'ight Dawg, holla at me tomorrow!"

I went back to look for ole girl and seen her looking for me also.

"I'm sorry, but I don't think we properly introduced ourselves, I'm L.C.!"

"Camille".

"Well, it's a pleasure to meet you Camille. Let's get outta here!"

We left the club, hopped on my bike and headed back to my place.

$$$

Lo is still in the club partying like a Rock Star, drinking up everything in the club and bouncing from chick to chick. He was so loose he didn't care who he was bumping into or whose woman he was snatching up. "Man watch where you steppin', Brah!" Lo shouted to this big linebacker looking nigga that looked like a Silverback Gorilla.

"Fool, watch where I'm steppin' or what?" He yelled walking up in Lo face. Lo took the half full bottle of Moet he had in his hand and smashed it across dude's face, leaving a gash from his eye down to his jaw bone. Blood was dripping everywhere as he fell to the floor holding his face. Women started screaming and making a scene and the bouncers came running from every angle. Lo slid outta the club and walked staggering back to his motorcycle drunk as hell. A squad car must've been watching him as he was coming out the club cause they rolled up behind him.

"Excuse me, sir!"

Lo act like he didn't even hear them say a word.

"Excuse me, sir!"

"Huh..."

"Are you okay?"

"Huh..?" Lo is so drunk he can't even understand what's going on.

"I said are you alright?"

"Uh huh." Lo nodded.

"Can I see your I.D. please?" Lo still kept his back turned to them, cause if he turned around and they see blood all over his clothes, it's going to be a "man down" situation. They walked up on him.

"Sir, are you drunk?" Lo nodded "no"

"Okay sir, I'm going to give you a standard alcohol screening. Can you say you're ABC's for me please?"

"Uh... A, Z, T, V, O, P, me!" They immediatly handcuffed him and took him to the downtown jail.

$$$

As soon as Camille and I entered the door of my crib, we were kissing like we were both some wild animals in heat; bumping into walls and tripping all over furniture. I led her into the kitchen and sat her on the counter top. I unbuttoned her shirt as I was placing soft kisses on her neck. Taking off her bra, I reached in the cabinet above and grabbed a can of whip cream. Putting silver dollar amounts on her chest, I began to suck it off as she moaned in ecstasy.

"Awwww!" I took my left hand and crawled it up her skirt inserting my ring and middle finger into her wet juices working her clit. Her body began to shake as she grabbed the counter top.

"Damn, baby. That's my spot!" she moaned. I put whip cream on her inner thigh, and started at her knees, kissing and licking; working my way up to her precious gates. Her eyes began to roll in the back of her head. It wasn't even three minutes, and she was grabbing on to my ears releasing her creams all on my tongue.

"God damn Daddy. You workin' that tongue!" she whimpered as I sucked on her clit, and began to thrust it into her tunnel of warmth.

Messaging my shaft, ready to perform, I put just an inch inside her soul and she started biting down on her bottom lip. I teased her continuously and by the look on her face, anticipation is driving her crazy. I gave her another inch of my shaft and she held her head back. Getting ready to fill her up, my house phone started ringing. "Who the hell is this calling me?" I thought. Not wanting to stop, I slide every inch of me inside of her and her mouth opened up wide.

"Aw f-fuck!" she bellowed. The phone was still ringing like hell and I couldn't ignore it by then so I pulled out and went to look at the caller I.D. and it read unavailable. "Who the hell is this?" I thought to myself. I put the phone back down and headed back to my freak show in the kitchen. The phone rang again and this time I was agitated. I ran back to the phone with my pants to my ankles walking like a damn penguin.

"Hello!" I yelled.

"You have a collect call from... "Lo". If you wish to accept this call, please press 1 now."

"Hello"

"Lo, what da hell is goin' on?"

"Man, I need you to come get me out". When he said that, I watched my piece go from eight to three in a matter of seconds.

"A'ight man, I'm on my way." I sighed and went back to the kitchen and told Camille I had to take care of something.

"Aw Daddy, you gon' leave me like this?" She looked down at her pussy and it was dripping on the counter like a sink with the knob barely on.

"I'm sorry baby but..." She pulled me close to her, grabbed my hand and started twirling it around on her clit.

"Aww....damn baby you tryna' make me weak huh?" I snapped out of it and backed off pulling my pants up.

On my way taking Camille home all I could think about was I don' let this girl get off and I didn't even come close.

"Ima call you okay?" I said, dropping her off.

"Yeah, make sure you do that." She said sarcastically. I drove off thinking, what the hell this nigga don' got into na'? This fool is always loose as hell. When I picked Lo up he came out with blood all over his clothes. I just shook my head as he explained what happened.

CHAPTER 6

I'm at the crib and it hit me that I haven't seen my mom in quite some time. She stays out in Taylor and I been so busy I haven't had time to drive out there. Me and my mom are real close, I am her first and only child, so we have that bond naturally. She couldn't have any more kids after me because of a rare blood disorder she has. Growing up she would always tell me I was the chosen one. At times growing up though, I always wanted brothers and sisters, but I guess pit bulls were the substitute for that because Willie always kept them around.

"Hey, what's up Ma?"

"Hey Baby, how you?" My mother still calls me "baby" and I'm twenty-eight years old.

"Nothing much, Ma. It smells good in here. What you cooking?"

"Oh, just a little chicken, eggs, waffles, and bacon."

"Damn Mama, I thought you said a little something". We started laughing.

"Where Willie at?"

Willie is my mom's husband; they got married when I was about eight years old. He and I never saw eye to eye and to this day, I keep my words short and brief.

"He left here not too long ago. You just missed him." Like I was looking for him anyway.

"Ima take the dog for a walk a'ight?"

"Okay Hun, don't be long!"

I go to this park where it's always women walking their dogs like clockwork, as soon as I got there, it was flooded.

"Excuse me, sir," a woman tapped me on my shoulder.

"Yes?" I was smiling cause it's always the same attention.

"Is that your dog?" referring to my mother's all white Poodle with a red scarf around the neck.

"Well, what if I said no?"

"Well, if you was to say no, then that would mean if we were to hook up my dog wouldn't have a date mate, and we wouldn't have much alone time!" She was smiling and I knew she was feeling me. She had the same kind of dog my mom had.

"Well…in that case this is my dog, and I'm L.C.!"

"Toya. Nice to meet you!"

"The pleasure is all mines!" Looking at this five foot nine, chocolate angel with a body like, America's Next Top Model. I mean she had a little nice petite booty that was poking outta her stretch pants like it was gasping for air, not to mention the Halle Berry haircut. She was flawless.

"Shall we continue to walk?" she suggested.

"Let's get it!"

An hour went by and we talked about everything under the sun. My mom was calling my phone.

"Hello?"

"Boy, what you don' did wit my dog?"

"Oh, she's alright. I'll be there in a minute".

I was cracking up looking at Toya cause I knew she could hear my momma yelling on the other end of the phone. I hung up the phone and Toya was grilling me. I haven't even known this girl for twenty-four hours and I'm lying already.

"Oh, so that isn't your dog after all, huh?" she said with a raised eye brow.

"Naw, naw, it's not, but I wasn't gone pass up the chance of getting to know you. You can't say you didn't have a good time with me today."

"Yeah you gotta point there."

"So when can I see you again, Ms. Toya?"

"Well, how about the next time you walk your mother's dog!" she said smiling, giving me her number and then and walking away.

"Wait! Hold on, baby girl, you serious?" She just turned around in her truck and gave me this look as if she wasn't playing.

I walked back to my mom's house and when I got there, Willie was there.

"What's up, Willie?"

"What's going on Leon, you alright?"

"Yeah man, just surviving that's all."

"How is the shop coming along?"

"Everything is everything. You know I can't complain. Hold on a second, I gotta call." I stepped outside… "Hey B what's up?"

"I'm down at the club and that guy you was asking me about just left. He was here with some other dude but they left at the same time, like thirty minutes ago."

"Oh yeah?"

"Uh huh!"

"Well a'ight, thanks for letting me know."

"We still hookin' up tonight?"

"Uh…" damn I forgot about that, "Uh..Ima call you a'ight?"

"Boy, whatever!"

"I'm serious. Ima call you later on tonight I gotta handle some paper work at my shop."

"Okay, Leon, I'll talk to you later". We hung up the phone and I went back in the living room and sat down. Willie brought his nosey ass back in there with me.

"Hey, Leon?"

"Uh huh?"

"You know your uncle supposed to get out soon, and he's been asking about you!"

"WHAT!" When he told me that, my heart jumped through my chest.

$$$

It was July 4th eighteen years ago, and everybody
from the family was at my house. Back then, we lived in the
projects out in Ecorse. The whole neighborhood was
jamming to this song by Marvin Gay , "Get Up and
Party….". As a youngsta, I always liked to be around grown
folks, especially my family. I knew that at any given time it
could be an argument or a fight. Even though family fighting
family is wrong, it sure as hell a good laugh just watching it.

"DOMINO!" My uncle yelled drinking a 40 oz. of
MGD. My uncle, Smitty, was a gangsta, well known all over
the city of Detroit. He was well respected by all kinds of
people: police, women, judges, pastors, congressmen, and
even white people. To me, he was just my uncle, but to the
world he was a 'G'. I looked over and saw my mom doing
her one, two step with her husband, and my grandmother and
grand dad were trying to show everybody younger than them
how they use to dance back in them Malcolm X days. All in
all, it was a good night in the projects.

"DOMINO!" my uncle yelled again at the table,
slamming the bone down when he's out. The look on

everybody else's face was disgusted because of him wining. Sometimes, I use to watch him play cards and he'd be cheating like hell, and everybody knew it, but was scared to say it.

"I'm through playing with ya'll sorry asses!" he yelled out and left the table.

"God dammit! You ain't through till you gimme a chance to win my money back!" one of the guys stood up and yelled out.

"GET PAID!!" Smitty shouted.

"Get paid? Oh, Ima get paid alright!"

My uncle just stood there starring at the guy as if he couldn't believe he was talking to him like that. Hell, I couldn't believe it either. Seconds later, my uncle walked in the house and I followed right behind him. He was in the bedroom and I could see him through the crack of the door loading up a gun. I walked in and my uncle turned around and starred at me.

"Boy, what you doing in here?"

"Nothing, I was just seeing if you need me to get anything for you." I replied, really not knowing what to say at that moment.

"Come here Boy. Sit right here," he gestured me to come sit next to him on the bed while he was still putting bullets in the gun. He showed me how to load it, aim it, and shoot. "Nephew, let me tell you something, if you ever get caught up with a gun or go to prison for anything, Ima kill you! I don't want you to get caught up in these streets. Before I let the streets get you, I'll get you my damn self. You hear me?"

As a ten year old I really didn't know how to take that, so all I could say was "What do you mean?"

"Just like I said, Nephew. I don't ever want you to get caught up with guns and end up going to prison, and if you ever do, I'ma kill you!" All I could do at that point was remain silent as he got up and left the room. I sat there still wondering if he would actually kill his own flesh and blood. I mean, family members fight each other, but do they kill each other?

Moments later, I heard arguing in the backyard. My uncle was talking to the one who he told to get paid.

"Fool, what da hell you mean? Ima get paid alright". BLOOM! BLOOM! BLOOM! BLOOM! BLOOM! BLOOM! My uncle emptied out every bullet he had in the gun into the chest of the man he got into it with and people was running everywhere. My uncle was so drunk he just stayed there until the police came and took him to jail.

He ended up getting life without the possibility of parole. I don' did two years in the joint for a pistol and just got out. It's going to be a real situation dealing with my uncle. I'm his nephew and all, but, to him, it seems like I'm another human being on this earth that doesn't matter. Oh well, I'll just worry about that later. I got my own problems to worry about, and besides, he ain't out now anyway.

"Leon".

"Oh..huh" I was daydreaming "My bad Ma, what's up?"

"You hungry?"

"Yeah, a little bit. You did cook a lot of food."

"Wash up and I'm going to fix you a plate."

I went to the bathroom to wash my hands and when I came out, my mom and Willie were sitting at the table eating. "Its some biscuits in the oven, if you want some. They should still be warm too." Mom pointed.

I looked in the oven and grabbed a few biscuits and sat down.

"So when was the last time you went to the church?" she asked.

"It's been a minute."

"You know you need to go and spend sometime with your grandfather."

"He asks about you all the time."

"I'll go see him one of these days. Maybe not at the church though, but one of these days."

"Ok Leon, don't act like you too good to go to church now."

"I hear you now." I said stuffing my face with eggs and bacon so I could hurry up and leave.

"Willie said his brother has been asking about you."

"I don't know why! What he asking for me for?" I looked at Willie and he hunched his shoulders as if he really did not know why. "I suppose you wouldn't tell me anyway huh?"

"Leon!" my mom yelled. "What is wrong with you?"

"Nothing Ma, I'm cool. Look, I gotta' go a'ight." I stood up and gave her a hug and a kiss on the cheek.

"You not gonna say bye to Willie?" She said as I was halfway out the door. She knows damn well I hate him with a passion, and if he was just a boyfriend I would have been put a bullet in him.

CHAPTER 7

I went home to chill out for a while, listening to some music, watching Sports Center and I just happen to look at my cell phone and noticed I had some missed calls. I knew something was odd cause my phone is usually always ringing off the hook. Ms. Becky had been tryna call me so I called her up.

"Hey, how you doing Ms. Becky?"

"Hey, what's up with you? I've been tryna call you for quite some time."

"Yeah, I was sitting here with the music blasting looking at the T.V. I must've been in a zone; I'm sorry."

"Yeah, you must have. What are you doing tonight?"

"I have nothing planned, what's up?"

"Well, I was wondering if you would like to come over for dinner. Are you hungry?"

"I can eat!"

"Well, come by let's say….8:30p.m.?"

"It's a date. See you then!"

I hung up the phone, turned the music up a little louder, and got ready.

Just as I was getting ready to walk out the door, I saw Tony running across the grass.

"Tony, what da hell are you doing here?"

"I-I need to uh…talk to you."

Tony was exhausted like he has been running for a minute. His shirt was full of sweat and he could barely stand up straight.

"Come inside." I motioned him and we sat on the couch. "What's the problem?"

"When I was in jail, I had this little situation with these guys I was gambling with. I lost a lot of money and told them I was gonna pay them when I got out."

"How much?"

"Nine hundred dollars"

"NINE HUNDRED DOLLARS! TONY! How the hell do you lose nine hundred dollars in a county jail?"

"It was rough man. I had to eat!"

"Well, why are you here?"

"I was at home and apparently they found out where I lived and showed up on my door step. That's when I shot out the back door and came here."

"Tony! Tony! Tony!" was all I could say looking at this little Hispanic kid scared for his life. I couldn't let him go back home for a while so I let him stay at my place for a couple of days.

"I can't chill and party with you tonight. I gotta a date to get to."

"A date with who?

"Ms. Becky"

"Oh yeah Ms. Becky, man she had a nice body on her!" Tony was looking at the ceiling rubbing his hands together as if Becky was sliding down a stripper pole or something.

"Make yourself at home, Tony. I'm out!" I said, heading out the door.

When I got to Becky's house, it was about 8:27 p.m. She opened the door and she had on this red dress that came down to the middle of her thighs. Her hair was straight down and she had on these red Prada glasses that made her look like a school teacher. Scented candles where lit throughout the house which smelled like cinnamon. The dinner table was already ready.

"Damn baby, you looking real good tonight!" I said

"Thank you!"

"Naw, thank you!" I replied, back looking at her up and down.

"I've been looking forward to this date since we met." she replied.

"Is that right? Well, I hope it doesn't end to soon."

"Well, if you play your cards right, then maybe it won't!" She said walking to the back of her condo. Watching her sashay across the room made me wanna pounce on her right then and there!

"Turn on some music!" she yelled from the back. I looked through her CD's to find the most seductive music that I could find, and wha-lah, "Dot com" by Usher. There couldn't be a better song for the moment.

Sitting across from each other, I could tell that it was a lot of anticipated emotion floating off her body. Looking into her deep blue eyes, I knew it was going to be a long night. I was trying to control myself so she wouldn't think this was all I wanted, but hell, this was all she wanted. I'll just play it out for a minute and see how things go.

$$$

Back at my place, Tony had become restless there by himself. He began to become paranoid knowing that somebody was looking for him. So, he decided to go outside and get some fresh air. He hadn't even walked a full block before he had gotten spotted. Just that quick, he ran as fast as he could to try and get away but once he ran into an alley, it was a dead-end and there was nowhere else to go.

He knew he was cornered so he just turned around and faced his enemy.

"Well, well, well, Tony"

"How did you find me here?"

"Oh, you thought you was gonna run forever? Man we know people. If you don't pay us then that means were are in debt, and we cant be in debt Tony."

"Wait! Man hold up." Tony put his hands in the air trying to stall hoping that someone would ride by and save him.

One of the guy's phone rung, and when he looked at who was calling he started smiling as he answered.

"Hello....yeah we got him right here....sure thing" he hung up the phone, and then the two guys walked up to Tony, grabbed him by his arm and drug him into there black suburban truck and drove off.

$$$

Dinner was over and I was a little full, but I still was ready for dessert.

"So, what's for dessert?" I was curious.

"Hold on a minute. Let me go slip on something more comfortable." She said leaving the table walking to the back room.

"L. C.!" she yelled moments later. "Can you come in here please? I need some help!"

When I walked into the bedroom she had the whole room lit with candles and she had a red light in the lamp on her nightstand that had the whole room looking like the Red Light District. A song by the Isley Brothers was playing through her little stereo system, "In between the sheets..."

She had on this pink lingerie laced in white and she was sitting on the bed. Her nipples were cut out the lingerie and they were just as pink as her garment. I took my shirt off and walked over to the bed and sat down. She got behind me and started rubbing my back and kissing the back of my neck, working her way around to my chest.

She pushed me down on my back and I was lying halfway on the bed with my feet on the ground and my dick hard as a 2x4. She straddled me and began to kiss and lick all over my six pack in between the lines. She unbuttoned my pants and pulled them down. My shaft was standing firm and long ready for action.

"Oh, I see you ain't half steppin at all!" she said.

When my shaft caught her undivided attention, she started licking the head and within seconds she had my whole eight inch dick in her mouth serving me up.

"Damn, baby. Gimmie dat Becky!" I whispered.

It was like she was an undercover porn star. She got up and grabbed a cup that was sitting on the night stand and put some water in her mouth. She got back in between my legs and when she put her mouth on my head I felt that it was hot water in her mouth; I skeeted as soon as her mouth touched me.

After waiting a few seconds before going back for another nut, I then turned her on her stomach and arched her back just enough to where my whole man could slide in her soul.

"Aw, damn baby it's in my stomach!" she cried.

I grabbed both of her butt cheeks and spread them apart and began to pound her like a mad man.

"Aw, Aw, Aw, Aw, Aw, … F-Fuck me!" She yelled as I had both of her cheeks in the palm of my hands. Slap….Slap….Slap….Slap….Slap….

"Oh, s-shit! Don't st-st- stop. I'm c-c-cum OOOhShit, Damn!"

Me and her both come at the same time. She had a towel next to her bed and I wiped the cum off her and laid down. She laid on my chest with her right leg across my body and we both fell asleep.

CHAPTER 8

I made it home about noon. After that freak episode with Becky I thought I'd just chill out a little bit. Damn, she had me going last night. She even had ah nigga some grits and eggs ready for me this morning. I can't fall for it though, not this time. I gotta do me for now, and now that my uncle bout to get out, I got more problems I'ma have to deal with later. "Who da hell is this calling me now?" It better not be Becky. "Hello!"

"What's up fool?"

"What's up, Tek. What's hood?"

"You feel like racing tonight?"

"Hell, yeah. How much?"

"Five stacks."

"Five stacks? Who da' hell tryna loose dat much?

"You know I'm always looking for dummies tryna' act like they Top Dollar out here."

"Alright bet! I'm on my way."

We hung up the phone and I immediately put on my jeans and headed out the door to my bike.

When I got to the bike race on Warren and Livernois, it was people everywhere; I mean it was jumping like never before.

When I met up with Tek, he was chillin' on his bike talking to some bad little Asian chick. I thought I was in Tokyo Drift.

"Wud up, Boy?"

"Wud up doe? See, you ain't waste no time in getting down here!"

"For five stacks, hell who wouldn't? Who is this?"

"I'm Itika!"

"Itika, huh?"

"That's right, Daddy!"

"Well Itika, let me talk to my boy real quick and we'll get at you later A'ight?"

She nodded her head, licked the blow pop sucker she had in her mouth, and walked into the crowd.

"Hm…hm…hm… where da' hell you find her at?"

"Nigga, she found me!"

"Aye, I need to holla at you about something Dawg on some real shit."

"What's up, Fam?"

"When I was at...

Somebody shouted walking toward Tek, were "da money at, homie?"

"Oh, we stay caked up ova here. You ready to race?"

Tek pulled out a brown liquor store bag that had the money in it. "It's all here, Dawg. I told you we caked up ova here!"

I'm looking at him and his crew, and you can tell when people not from the city. Detroit has it's own distinctive swag.

"So, are we gonna race or what?" I yelled.

"You ain't said nothin' but a word."

I grabbed my helmet and started walking towards my bike.

"What were you about to say homie?" Tek asked.

"Man, I gotta serious problem on my hands, Dawg and I need some advise on this one."

"A'right well....win this easy ass money real quick and then we gon' chop it up." He said given me some dap.

We pulled up to the start line and this caramel toned woman with long hair, stood in between us with a towel in her hand. I put my helmet on and looked back up and it was that Asian chick Tek was just hollering at.

"I got this one, Rita!" she told the woman taking the towel outta her hand and holding it in the air.

I looked at my opponent and he looked at me. We nodded our heads and started to rev our bikes up.

"On your mark!"

In my mind I'm thinking, "I can't lose five stacks, I can't lose five stacks!"

"Get Set!"

I looked at Tek and he nodded his head letting me know I got this.

"GO!!"

We took off racing down the street flying. I haven't lost a race yet and I knew I couldn't lose one now. I had a good lead on him by the time we got to the middle of the block then he started catching up to me.

Just before we were about to cross the finish line, a stray dog came across the street and ran in front of him; he swerved out the way and flipped off his bike, rolling about eighty yards.

When I passed the finish line, I rode back to Tek, and waited for the other guy to return. I seen him limping back towards us and by the look on his face he was pissed.

"Time to pay up, Homie!" Tek said to him as he walked up.

"Man, I ain't paying you a damn thing. Ya'll cheated!"

"Nigga, how da' hell we cheat you?"

"You ain't see that damn dog run across the road?" he said pointing up the street.

"Homie dat ain't had nothing to do wit us. Either you pay up or its…"

"Or what?", the man cut Tek off and stepped to his face.

"Or dis nigga…"

Tek pulled out a .357 and pointed it at his head. Obviously, Tek picked the right person to race as always cause he ain't do nothing but back up and threw the money at Tek and left. Dem niggas must not be from round here, cause in the D everybody gotta bang.

We busted out laughing as they dipped off through the crowd.

"He act like he was really bout to do something!" Tek said.

"Hell yeah, till he saw dat heater, then that nigga started sweatin' bullets!" I replied back.

We laughed at what just happened till I noticed this familiar face around a group of females. I knew I knew her from somewhere, but couldn't put my finger on it. As I got closer the face became familiar to me.

"Camille?" I questioned.

"It's me L.C., how have you been? I haven't heard from you in a while."

"I've been doing okay. I seen you racing tonight. You was looking good out there. When can I go for another ride?"

"You can ride right now if you wanna."

I pulled her up close to me grabbing her waist.

"I'll be right back. Let me go holla at my boy real quick."

I went to look for Tek and he was all hugged up on that Asian chick again.

"Aye Homie, I'm bout to bounce. You good for tonight?"

He looked at the Asian chick then back at me.

"Yeah, I'm good, Dawg. Make sure you get at me tomorrow, a'ight?"

We gave each other dap and as I was walking back to meet up with Camille all I heard was GLAH! GLAH! GLAH! GLAH! Somebody was choppin' the block up. People started running everywhere and I grabbed ole girl up and we took off. The only thing in my mind at this point was, "I'm not going to be left out this time!" I took her to Belle Isle and we got it in.

The next morning I woke up, cut the T.V. on, and went in to the bathroom. Brushing my teeth, I heard the Fox 2 News on. They were talking about a shooting that took place last night over on Livernois.

'Last night a shooting took place on Livernois leaving the victim in critical condition at the Henry Ford Hospital.'

I poked my head out to get a better understanding about what was going on, but they changed the subject to the weather, so I kept brushing my teeth, and then...

'Breaking news, police just identified the victim as Tekno Roberts!'

When I heard Tek's name I ran to the TV and they were at the scene of the shooting. His bike was all scratched up and they had caution tape all around the block.

I called his cell phone just to see if I was hearing this right.

"Yo' Wud dup doe, dis Tek; LEAVE IT!" his damn voice mail came on the first ring; I through my clothes on and headed to the hospital.

CHAPTER 9

When I got here, Tek was still unconscious. The doctor said that the bullet hit a main artery and he might not make it. I'm sitting here looking at him with all these tubes running through his body.

"Tek, wake up for me, Man. I know you hear me, Dawg. Look man, I'ma take care of it a'ight?"

He just laid there breathing threw the tube in his mouth as if he didn't even feel me standing there. I walked outside the door and tried to make a phone call. I didn't have a signal so I went outside and called up Big Ray.

"Big Ray, wud dup?"

"L.C., my man, what's hood?"

"Man somebody tried to kill Tek last night!"

"WHAT!? Get the hell outta here, STRAIGHT UP!?"

"Yeah, man, and I think I know who did it."

"Well say the word, Dawg!"

I already know how Big Ray roles, so that was all I had to hear him say.

We hung up the phone and not even twenty seconds after that my cousin was calling.

"What's up, Lo?"

"What's up, Cuz?"

"Nothing much I'm…"

"You seen Tony lately?" He cut me off.

"Naw, why you ask me that?"

"Man, the word around the hood is some nigga kidnapped a young Hispanic kid over some money he owed them from jail. I don't know much about the money part, but young, Hispanic, and jail fit the description of Tony and I wanted to make sure it wasn't him."

"I don't know man. I'ma call the shop and see if he's there, he should be."

"A'ight, man. Hit me right back!"

This is just too much for a nigga in one day.

"SO-G Barber, Hair and Nail Salon, Andell speaking, how…"

"Auntie, is Tony there?"

"Naw, nephew, I haven't seen him in a couple of days. I thought maybe he quit or something."

"Dammit, man!"

"What's wrong, Leon?"

"Nothing, auntie, I'ma' call you back."

When we hung up the phone all I could do was just think about going back to prison. I ain't tryna go that route again but if need be, give me a one way ticket cause I'm going all out. One thing about me, is that if I'm down for you, I'ma' ride for you till the death of me. That's a trait many niggas out here don't have. It's only a handful.

I called the one person who I knew I could get the best advice from. My Grandfather.

"Hey Granddad, what's up?"

"Hey Grandson, what's going on?"

"Nothing much I need to talk to you about something."

"What's that?"

"For some reason I think I'm falling back into my old ways just like before I went to prison. I'm feeling anger, rage, and every other feeling I felt before then. Why is that?"

"Well Grandson, you know that's what happens when you leave the church. The devil is a lot busier when church folk backslide. That's like his way of feeling like he won you over and when he feels like that, that's how he wants to keep it."

"I know I know. So, what do I do?"

"There's only one thing you can do, Grandson, and that's pray. All of your questions will be answered. You been in the church since you were a little boy. You should know that…"

"Alright, Granddad. Thanks for the talk."

"Okay, I'll be looking forward to seeing you soon!"

"Alright, bye."

We hung up the phone and as I began to get down on my knees the only thing on my mind was revenge. They done tried to kill my #1 man, and my little homie came up missing. My grandfather was right. It seemed like every since I stop going to church my life did a complete 180 degree turn. I started going closer and closer to Hell's direction. I was once told that you can become a devil over night. By me understanding a devil is one who uses deceptive intelligence that rationalizes disobedience to the will of God, whose evil only affects himself and not some red man with a tail and pitchfork. I knew that very minute, I had become just that. It wasn't no denying it because I clearly understood the very essence of the situation at hand, and because I understood the root of the problem, I immediately started praying.

"Dear God--"

My phone broke up my prayer and it was Lo calling back.

"Hello?" I answered

"They got him, Dawg!"

Just that fast, I went from talking to God, to accepting advise from Lucifer.

"A'ight, I'm on my way!" I hung up the phone and went home to grab my black .45 and headed to Lo's house in Brightmoore; a neighborhood known for some of the most grimiest, deceitful, careless people over all of Detroit. Just thinking about it made me go back in the house and grab my 12 gauge.

When I got to his crib on Kane Street he was standing on the porch as usual, in a wife beater.

"What up cuz? Red-rum is the only thing I'm thinkin about now!"

"Yeah, I hear you man. You know where the spot at?"

"Yeah let's ride by there real quick!"

We rode by the crib that they apparently had Lil Tony. It was the first house next to this old elementary school that was closed down on Bramell.

"Dat look like a damn spot house," I said to Lo. "Well, we can go chill for right now and wait till tonight." I suggested.

We went back to Lo's house and started getting some liquor in our system and smoked some weed. I told him about everything that happened with Tek and when night time came, it was time to ride out.

We hopped in one of Lo's all black Tahoes and headed to our destination. All the lights were off at the spot house and people kept walking to and from the back of the house. This must be busy hours and we didn't even care.

When we got close up on the house we could see a light on in the back room. We hid on the side this old abandoned house that was next to it and we saw a guy walk to the back of the house.

"Dat's the nigga right there!" Lo whispered in my ear.

Come to think of it, it look like the same nigga I seen at the bike races, the same nigga who probably shot my nigga, Tek.

I ran from the side of the house to the spot house. We walked to the back and I saw a few dog houses, but no dogs.

When I looked through the window, I could see him sitting on a bed with a woman in between his legs. He was rolling up a blunt look like.

"It looks like it's just them two in the house, but where da hell Tony at?" I asked.

"What's the plan, Cuz?" Lo wondered.

"Just follow me," I demanded.

I opened the screen door holding on to the springs trying not to make much noise. Lo followed up right behind me. The room the guy was in was in the next room over, and I could hear a customer coming to his window, me and Lo stayed still in the kitchen till they left.

When we heard the window shut, we tip toed to the room door.

"On the count of three!" I whispered.

"1…2…3…DON'T MOVE!" I yelled.

"You remember me Homie? He looked at me hard then he finally realized.

"Man, I swear I had nothing to," Plop! I slapped him across the mouth with the butt of the .45 and he fell over bleeding holding his jaw.

"Now, Ima give you to the count of three to answer my question and the longer you take to answer, Ima start with her then finish with you!"

"Come on, man, don't do this!" he pleaded, spitting out blood.

"Where's da boy at?"

"One!"

"Please don't—"

"TWO!"

"What B—"

"THREE..." I yelled, not even giving him a chance, then Lo pulled the trigger and put a bullet in the woman's head, splattering blood all over the wall.

"Okay, okay,....okay!!" the man put his bloody hands in the air surrendering.

"Talk!" I yelled again.

"He's around the corner on Lamphere, at the corner house! An all white house, please don't shoot me!" he pleaded still spitting out blood. From the looks of it, I knocked back a few of his teeth.

"Swear to God, Man, if you lying to me!" I pulled the four pound bar back.

"I swear, Man. I'm not lyin'!" he said putting his hands up with his eyes closed.

"Lo, you stay here and Ima go around the corner. If anything goes wrong, you know what to do."

"A'ight Cuz!"

I left and headed to the spot I was told that Tony was. When I crept up to the window, I saw two Jamaican-looking cats with dreads, sitting at the dinner table drinking forties. This had to be the right spot, so I called Lo.

"Cuz?"

"Wassup?"

"I think this the house."

Through the phone, I heard Lo put three bullets to the guy.

"A'ight, I'm on my way!"

He met me in the back of the house, and I told him what was up.

"It's two dudes sitting at the table. They look like they drunk as hell. The window opens right here, we gon' go in this way, follow me."

We went through the window and waited a few seconds to get ourselves together. I cocked my gun back and headed to the front.

Glah! I shot one of the guys in the left leg just to let them know I wasn't playing and that I meant business. The other guy tried to grab his pistol until Lo came behind me with the gauge ready to unload.

'Hold on, be easy!" Lo shouted with the gauge pointed at him.

"Now Ima give ya'll niggas one chance to answer this question and ya'll try your luck. Where's da little boy ya'll kidnapped?

"What!" One of them yelled. "What boy?"

"You know exactly what the hell I'm talking about. The little Hispanic kid."

Lo raised the gauge.

"Wait! No listen, Man. I don't know what you talking about Homie."

I looked at Lo and he looked at me. We both wanted to pop off right then and there, but we still would be ignorant to the fact of where Tony was at, so killing these clowns would not help us at all.

"Nigga....GLAH!" I shouted as I shot him in the leg. The bullet I put in him must have been heating up on his ass, cause' it was written all over his face.

" GOD DAMMIT MAN!" he yelled in pain rocking back and forth holding his leg.

These niggas looked confused as hell, so did me and Lo. I knew that that fool around the corner couldn't have lied, unless he knew he was bout' to die anyway, and telling us a bogus story was going to be his way of buying more time on earth. Little did he know that time on earth cant be bought. If you cant justify your existence of being here on this planet, then it is what it is.

"Just tell me where he is man, that's it, and we will be on our way." I was irritated and tired of talking.

It seems like I am not getting anywhere with this and the trigger is getting lighter and lighter and my tolerance is running low.

Nobody said a word they just acted like some tough asses. They looked at each other then back at me. One of the guys was looking past me and Lo towards the basement. He acted like he wanted to say something.

"Lo, go check downstairs!"

Just as soon as Lo went downstairs he came back throwing up.

Blocka! Blocka! Blocka! Blocka! He let out four bullets, two to the one I shot and two to the other.

"Man, what you do that for?"

"When I went downstairs, it was a bag over the head of a body with a bullet through the head."

"What?" he downstairs dead.

I dropped down to my knees in shock like "damn". They didn't even give the little nigga a chance.

Moments later we hurried up out the spot, hopped in the truck and took off.

"Damn, man what the fuck!" I yelled. "This shit is just too much for a nigga right now straight up!" I was raging with fire over them killing Tony, but I still had another situation to handle. I don't need Lo on this one though so I'ma' cut him loose.

CHAPTER 10

When I dropped my cousin Lo off, I drove to the
hospital to check on Tek. I walked in the room and his head
was propped up and the TV was on. His eyes are halfway
open and he still had the tubes in his mouth drinking his
liquids.

"Hey Tek, what's up baby?"

He just looked at me cause he is still unable to talk. I
looked around the room and grabbed a chair and pulled it up
to his bed.

"Man it's been some crazy shit going on in these
streets man. He just looked me in the eyes waiting on my
next words. Little Tony was killed. Some little niggas
kidnapped him over a debt he owed from when he was in jail.

Me and Lo got there too late. I didn't see him though, but Lo said when he went down stairs to where Tony was, it was a bullet in his head with a bag over it."

Tek just shook his head with his eyes closed.

"I know man, I know, but we took care of it though. So, now it's on to the next one. Besides that, what the hell happened to you?"

He opened his eyes and balled his fist and put his arms in the air as if he was riding a motorcycle. The only thing I can think of was that it was the nigga that he pulled the burner out on the other night that came back and chopped the block up.

"A'ight, Dawg, listen, Ima take care of him, don't worry. Ima handle this alright?"

He just nodded his head. I guess he was saying he didn't want me to go, but I had to get back, and the way I'm feeling, I'm at the point of no return! It is what it is!

I left the hospital on my way to my bike races, I called Big Ray.

"Wud up doe?" he answered.

"Big Ray, It's time to rock out!"

"Say the word, Homes."

"Meet me at the Coney Island on Tireman and Livernois"

"A'ight, I'm on my way"

We hung up the phone and I headed to the Coney.

By the time I got there, Big Ray was already sitting down at the back table, and it looked like he had somebody with him. I walked in and went to the back, and pulled up a chair.

"Wud up, who dis?" I asked, Big Ray giving him a five and a half shoulder hug.

"Oh dis is my cousin, Doo Whop!"

"What's up Homie?" I said, giving him the same love. We all sat down at the table and leaned in toward the middle so our words wouldn't carry across the room. In a low voice, Big Ray started talking.

"Man I got a plan for how we gon' get at Dawg tonight so we can execute this situation, and come out alive."

"I'm listening." I said.

"That's why I got my little cousin with me. He gutta and willing to ride at any case!"

"Hell Yeah!" Doo Whop uttered.

"All you gotta do is just follow his lead, and everything should run as smooth as a baby's foot."

"Alright, well let's jump to it." I said.

Big Ray told me the play; we smoked a blunt, and left the Coney Island heading to the bike races.

Doo Whop looked like he was about sixteen years old. He was from the East Side of Detroit, over there by Chene, and we all know what kind of killas they breed over in that neck of the woods. He was skinny, and black as hell, with long braids. He almost look like Lil Boosie, with gold teeth. You would think that they were related.

I put my black mask under my helmet and Big Ray and Doo Whop was right behind me.

When we pulled up it was people everywhere. We parked our bikes and blended in with the crowd. I kept my helmet on so nobody could see my face. Somebody might remember me from a few days ago. I scoped the area looking for Dawg.

"Hey you?"

"What's up Itika."

"Where your boy at?"

Apparently she couldn't have been with Tek after they left last night, otherwise she would have knew, so I didn't bother telling her. As far as I know, she could have had a part in it.

"He ahh….chillin' tonight back at the crib."

"Well you tell him to call me ok?"

"A'ight."

She turned around and walked into the crowd.

"Man, who is that?" Doo Whop asked.

"This lil Asian chick Tek has been messing with."

"GOD ....DAMM SHE STRAPPED."

We both looked at her from behind until I looked up. This nigga had the nerve to really show up.

"Alright, there that nigga go right there." I signaled with my elbow. I acted like I was scratching my head to point him out.

"I'm on it!" Doo Whop said.

"I'm right behind you." Big Ray said, walking behind Doo Whop.

Big Ray made his way next to our target unnoticed and waited for Doo Whop to do his thing. Doo Whop with a little staggering walk in his strut, as if he was drunk or something, had money in a brown paper bag in his right hand and his helmet in his left.

"Who wanna race me?" Holding up the money in the air.

Everyone's attention went towards him. They were all looking like, "Who the hell is this little nigga?" He was putting on a show.

"Yeah, yeah, tha-tha-that's right" he was slobbering. "Ten stacks, who want it?"

Our target paid him no attention so he walked up on him and tapped him on the shoulder.

"Man what the hell you doing boy?" He turned around reaching for his pistol until he figured out that Doo Whop wasn't no threat.

Doo Whop put the money in his face.

"I know you want some of this."

"Boy, you just a kid. Shouldn't you be at home getting ready for school or something? Get the fuck outta here." He turned his back.

Doo Whop started laughing and I was just amazed at how this little nigga was performing. Like I said East Side Chene produces some of the best. He didn't give up though. He just kept forcing his hand.

"I'm just tryna get you to co-come up real quick."

"Man quit playing and take this lil kids money. He wanna play wit the Big Boys. Teach him a lesson and put him back in his place," Big Ray chimed in.

"Alright, I'll race you."

He walked up to Doo Whop.

"But when I win, I want yo bike, and the money. You wanna play with the Big Dawgs' right? Well let's play!"

He grabbed his helmet and hopped on his bike. Doo Whop looked at me, nodded his head, and hoped on his bike. They pulled up to the start line, and began revving their bikes. The flag went up, and right back down, and they took off down the street at full throttle.

I took off from a different angle that way I could meet them half way. By the time they got halfway down the street Doo Whop slowed down and I pulled out my .45.

I got a little closer to him… Plop! And shot his back tire. He started swerving out of control and ended up droppin' off his bike, sliding down the street side ways. He slid into this light pole, stomach first and fell back onto his back. I rode my bike to where he was and jumped off. He tried to take his helmet off and I ran towards him with a crow bar in my hand and smacked him across the head with it. He started screaming like a newborn baby, shaking like a fish out of the water. I pulled out the .45 Plop! Plop! Plop! I let him have it in the skull making sure he wouldn't live.

"L.C., let's ride!" Big Ray yelled, looking behind him cause everybody was starting to run toward our way to see what happened. I looked at Dawg one last time and nodded my head, a job well done. The smooth killa' strikes again.

I hopped on my bike and we all took off. We split ways after that and I headed to the hospital to tell Tek the good news. Visiting hours was over so I'ma sleep in the lobby until morning come back around.

$$\$\$\$$$

"Girl you did what?"

"I took a bat and I went to work on his new car."

Laughing.

Maria was at All-stars kicking it with her sister Tammie. This was the first time she had a chance to tell her since she got into with L.C.

"I told you girl. He ain't no good."

"I know Tammie, but I love him though that's my papi."

"Papi, huh? Yeah, ok Maria you better be careful, you already smashed his car up. You better be lucky he ain't beat the hell out of you for doing it."

Maria looked up and it was a guy standing behind Tammie. Once Tammie noticed Maria looking behind her.

"Yes" she said as she turned around.

"How much you charge for a song baby?"

He was rough looking in the face, not very attractive at all and Tammie was very picky when it came to certain men she would dance with.

"I'm sorry, but I'm on break right now."

"Oh, so what, you don't wont non' of this?" he pulled out a knot of money, flicking back hundred dollar bill, after hundred dollar bill.

"Sorry" she said like the money didn't fade her at all.

"Well what about you baby girl?" he looked at Maria.

Maria didn't have the look of a stripper, but I guess he was tryin' his luck with her. Maria didn't say anything, so he took it as if it was very negotiable and sat down next to her.

"Girl I'll be back." Tammie told Maria before getting up and leaving.

"So what's your name?" he ask her.

"Maria"

"Maria?" his eyes got big as he coughs after sipping on his drink.

"Yeah, why you say it like that?"

"Tonight must be my lucky night." He smiled and took another sip of his drink.

$$$

Morning rolled back quick, and after tossing and turning all damn night, I couldn't wait until visiting hours started again.

"Excuse me, Sir!" The lady behind the corner said to me.

I looked up. "Yes?"

"You can go up and see him now."

"Okay, thank you." I got up and went to his room.

I walked in and the tubes was out his mouth

"What's up baby?" I yelled as I walked in the room.

He turned and faced me. "What's up Dawg? What's hood?"

"Nothin', homie, I see you back alive, and why the hell are you in here watching "All My Children?" We both started laughing.

"Man, the nurse put it on that station. I was watching "Cheers" We started back laughing again.

"Like that's any better. Man, I thought the news said you were in critical condition?"

"Man, you know you can't believe what the Detroit News tell you. You know they just be trying to put a story together."

"True." I nodded. "You know I took care of that situation for you."

"What situation?" He asked with a confused look on his face.

"The nigga from the bike races; He the one that shot you ain't it?"

He put his hands on his face… "NAAAWW… man it wasn't him!!"

"WHAT? What the hell you mean it wasn't him?"

"Man look, remember that morning I called you when somebody shot my ride?"

I nodded.

"It was the same nigga. I was on my bike at a light on Six mile and Livernois, and a truck rolled up beside me. The light turned green and I took off down Six mile, but the truck caught up to me and starting shooting. He caught me twice in the back and I lost control of the bike and fell off. I hit my head on the ground first hard as hell. He caught me again in my left shoulder. I had my vest on so the two in the back didn't come through, but the one in my shoulder hit me hard. I tried to bust back but the impact had me going unconscious."

"So let me get this straight. You telling me I don' killed somebody and I didn't have to?"

"Man, I tried to talk to you last night but all I could do was shake my head."

I sure hope people don't recognize my bike last night otherwise I'ma' have a hard case to beat in court.

"Well anyway, glad you back Dawg fo' real cause I thought I lost you."

We gave each other a pound on the fist.

"Excuse me." The nurse knocked on the door. "You are free to go now."

Tek got his things together and I helped him walk to my bike. My crib wasn't far from the hospital so I rode there to get my car instead.

In the car on the way to Tek's house...

"A man, I need to talk to you about something."

"What's up, Dawg?"

"I think my uncle Smitty is on his way home soon."

"Oh yeah, you told me about him, that's a good thing ain't it?"

"Not quite, see, I didn't tell you everything about him. When I was younger he told me that if I ever caught up carrying a pistol and went to prison that he was going to kill me. He said he would kill me before the streets did."

"Man get the hell outta here, you serious?" Tek thought I was joking.

"Hell yeah, straight up! He's been asking about me lately."

"So you telling me that yo' own uncle, flesh and blood, would actually kill his own nephew?"

"Man, I don't know what to think but I ain't gon' let this fool rock me to sleep."

"I feel you, Dawg." Tek said coughing from the blunt we were smoking.

"Well, if you need me for anything you know I'm here for you. You know that right?"

"Yeah since Day One!"

"A'ight, man, I'ma' get in this crib and get myself together." Tek got out the car and walked up to his porch.

"L.C.!" He shouted

"What's up?"

"I'm here for you, homie." He said, then proceeded into the house.

I sat there for a minute thinking to myself if my uncle was trying to kill me would I shoot first? Either kill or be killed is what the streets teach you. All these thoughts began to take place in my head. I'm finishing off the blunt that me and Tek was smoking, while my mind is going a hundred miles and hour.

It seems like when you smoke weed you either paranoid, hungry, or just in a zone. Oh well, I'll worry about him later. I popped T.I's CD "Paper Trial" in, and put on my favorite song, "Ready for Whatever," and rode out down Joy Rd.

Chapter 11

"Nawll you gon' stay right here and do what I tell you to do"

Doo Whop was on the corner of Chene and Mack in front of the grocery store working, tryin' to make some sales. He hardly goes to school and when he does go, it's just to make a sale or two. He got a crew of young niggas that look up to him like he's a God or something. I guess when you know that a God is someone who is the Omnipotent Force, Power and Energy and not some spooky spirit floating around in the air, you began to take life on whole new hype.

"Man, why I gotta' stay here by myself and they get to go with you?" One of his toy soldiers complained.

"You wanna make some money don't you or do you want to go to school and let them teach you how to work a nine to five?"

The toy soldier nodded his head looking at the wad of money Doo Whop pulled out.

"Well act like it nigga!" Doo Whop hollered.

Doo Whop learned the streets at a early age when his mother and father was killed in drug deal gon' bad. The state tried to put him in a foster home but he kept running away. Every time they caught him, he would find a way to make his move out. Some white family out of West Bloomfield adopted him, come to find out it was his Big Homie from the hood who paid them to do it. Once they took Doo Whop out of the foster home they have not seen him since. Money will make you do some strange things in a recession if you know hat I mean.

"By the time I come back make sure yall have made about $250, nothing less a'ight."

"When you coming back?"

"30 minutes."

"30 MINUTES!"

"Yeah, fool 30 minutes. I gotta move quick, so make that money."

Doo Whop was notorious for taking hits for people. It didn't matter who it was to be killed cause' everybody's head had a price tag on it and for Doo Whop he only needed a few hundred and it was done. He was still in pursuit in finding out who killed his parents. He had the notion that if he sold enough drugs in the streets and made a big name for himself, that maybe he would eventually run into them. Not a bad idea for a 16 yrs old, but it has already been 5 ½ yrs since their death. He is still looking and ready to get back.

"Get that money JJ." Doo Whop said walking off with two of his soldiers to do a hit.

$$$

I stayed in the crib for a while cause everything that took place over the past week had me at an abnormal state of mind. I haven't been to my mothers or the strip in a week, so ima get out and go visit my mom today, and see what's up with her.

"What's up, Ma?"

"Hey Son, how are you?"

"I'm doing fine. I haven't seen you in a while, what's been going on?"

"Nothing much really, day to day problems as usual you know. Willie said your uncle been asking about you."

"Oh yeah? I wonder what he wants."

"I don't know"

" I'm about to take the dog for a walk."

"Okay, hun, see you in a bit."

When I left outta the house all I could think about was why the hell my uncle keeps asking about me.

I took my mom's dog to the same park I always go to, and was hoping to see Toya there. I haven't called her since the first day we met. I walked around the park a couple times till I saw her standing by her car talking to some Pookie look alike from New Jack City. I waited a while to see if they were saying their good-bye's, but that didn't work out. It looked like they were having too good of a conversation. So, I figured I'll go over and introduce myself.

When I walked up close they stopped talking and their eyes began to focus on me.

"Toya, it's me L.C.!"

"L.C.? Oh the L.C. that never called me back right?"

"Yeah, that's me! I've been having a lot of issues with my family that I had to take care of lately.

"What's up Homie? I'm T!" The Pookie look alike put his hand out to give me some dap, but I just looked at him like he was crazy.

"Ms. Toya, do you mind if we go somewhere and talk?"

"Yo, Dawg she wit me!"

I gave him a look saying if you say one more word.

"Did you…" POP! I slapped that boy so hard he flew off his feet into the air and on to his back.

"Yeah, you say what now?" I stood over him while he was laying there holding his mouth. Toya went to pick him off the ground.

"L.C., just leave!" Toya yelled.

I backed off him then my cell phone started to ring.

"What's up, Tek?"

"Wud up doe? What's hood?"

"Nothing, man just took care of some light work." I said giving him a kick in the rib cage.

"Listen, it's suppose to be a big party tonight at the State Theater. Dem boys from Rock Bottom suppose to show up so you know it's going to be banging. That fool that tried to kill me might even be there. You down?"

"You know I'm down Homie. Let's get it! I just gotta make one more run right quick so I'll be there a lil later, a'ight?"

"A'ight!"

I hung up the phone an headed back to my mom's house to drop her dog off cause I had to run to the shop real quick.

As soon as I entered the door to the shop all heads turned towards me. "What's up wit ya'll? Ya'll look like ya'll seen a ghost or something."

I looked over the room and saw Maria sitting in my auntie's chair getting her hair done. I walked to my auntie's chair and acted like I didn't see her.

"What's up, auntie?"

"Hey, nephew, how you been?"

"I've been alright, just chillin."

"You got some mail at your desk."

"A'ight."

I walked past Maria as if she wasn't even there. I walked in the office and sat down for a minute. Seconds later, I heard bells on the front door open and everybody in the shop got quiet again. I looked through the blinds and see that it's Becky sitting at the waiting table tryna get her nails done.

"Dammit!" I said to myself, knowing that it was about to be mad drama in about ten minutes.

"Andell, is that it?" I yelled.

"Yeah, that's it. Can you come here for a minute?"

I think my auntie wants to see a show so she called me to the front knowing that Becky gonna be all up on me in front of Maria. Oh well, it don't matter anyways I know how to handle these situations.

I walked out the back office and Becky was heading to my direction. I guess when my auntie yelled she knew I was there.

"How you doin', Becky?" I had no choice but to put my arms up and hug her cause her arms were stretched out from the beginning.

"Hey, Baby, how are you?"

"I'm good, you about to get your nails done?"

"Yeah, for you tonight!"

Why she said that, I don't know. I looking at Maria through the mirror and I could tell she was getting hot. I tried to creep back into the office before Maria would say something, but too late!

"So is this the trick you cheated on me with?"

"Trick, who you calling a trick?" Becky said shouting back.

"I'm just callin' em' like I see em'!"

Maria started walking up on Becky and I couldn't stand there and watch any longer, so I stood between them.

"Maria, what's yo damn problem?"

"Oh so, this is how you doing me, Leon?"

"I don't have nothing to explain to you, Maria, You ain't my woman no more. So what's the deal?"

"So that's how it is, huh?"

"Naw, that's how it's gon' be."

I grabbed Becky by the hand and led her out.

"I'm sorry about that, my ex is just jealous. She's not with me anymore."

"You don't have to explain anything, I understand!"

"Am I still going to be able to see you tonight?"

"Of course, just gimme a call when you done with her okay?"

"No problem."

Becky went on her way and I went back in the shop to deal with Maria. I took her in my office.

"What the hell is your problem? Who you think you are checking up on me?"

"Oh so I'm a stalker now?"

"You hadn't been here in three months and all of a sudden I guess you just gone decide to show up huh?"

"I miss you, Papi. Don't you miss me?"

"You miss me, huh?"

"I've been missing you since the day I left you."

She started walking up on me, tryna kiss me, but I pushed her back.

"Why you acting like that, Leon? Come here, Papi!"

She sat on my lap, and I felt my cell phone vibrating. I threw her off and took my phone call.

"What's up, Baby?"

"L.C., I need to tell you something important."

"What's up?"

"Remember when you came in here and said you noticed somebody looking at you from the back of the club?"

"Yeah."

"Well he's coming here more often, and he's been asking about you."

"What has he been saying?"

"He just been wanting to know if I talked to you and when you coming back? You sure you don't know who it is?"

"Naw, I couldn't tell, but don't worry, A'ight?"

"Okay."

By the time we hung up the phone Maria had left out the shop. I guess she heard Bamby's voice on the other end. Oh well, I'm trying to figure out who this clown is that's looking for me. I'll find out later because if he was looking for me like that, he'll be right there when I get there.

I look on the couch and see a napkin with some red writing on it. I picked it up and it read, "You gon' get yours sooner than you think!" I think it was written in the same red lipstick that Maria had on.

I ran outta the office. "Auntie where Maria at?"

"She just left out the door."

When I got outside she was pulling off listening to the same Kelis song "I'm Bossy."

CHAPTER 12

We riding by the State Theater on Woodward and it's off da hook. The line is so long they have two lines, one for people just tryna get in and a line for couples only.

We parked across the street in front of Comerica Park and walked over. We scooped a couple ladies along the way and got in the line. I got my pistol in my Timberland boot and I'm sure Tek got his.

Just our luck Big Ray is working tonight. I guess when it's big events they call him cause they know he don't got a problem with moving any furniture if something goes down.

"What's up L.C., Tek? Come straight through."

We walked through the doors and Big Sean's song was subbing through the speakers loudly. "I Do It….Boi"

We walked straight up to the bar.

"Let me get four bottles of Corona's." I told the bartender.

"Coming right up!"

She bought our drinks back and we started sipping, not really trying to get drunk cause the only thing on our mind was execution.

"You see him yet?"

"Naw, not yet, but I'm lookin', and when I do, its curtains."

I glanced up on the upper deck and noticed this lady in red grilling me. She signaled me to come up to where she was.

"Aye, Dawg, I'll be right back."

"A'ight, Dawg, go for it." I went upstairs to holla at this cold cut piece. "

"Hi. How are you?" she greeted me as I approached her.

"I'm fine how are you doing? I'm King!"

I threw an alias at her cause soon as I see Tek move, I'm out.

"I'm doing better now that you came up! I'm Kita."

"Nice to meet you Kita". I'm looking at her and focusing on Tek at the same time.

"Are you here by yourself?" she asked me.

"As a matter of fact I am, Are you?"

"Not anymore." She whispered in my ear.

I took a sip of beer and the Detroit rap group Rock Bottom started rapping their song.

"Rule number one... You betsta' have yo gun...Rule number two...You betsta' duck and shoot.....recognize bitch the dirty mitten"

"Why so shy?", she asked me.

"I'm not shy at all, Sweetheart. I just don't have enough liquor in my system yet."

From downstairs she looked like Beyonce', but up close she look like Whoopi Goldberg.

"Well, have a sip of this." She tried to give me her glass of whatever she was drinking.

"Naw, that's okay, I'll just sip on these for a lil while."

Holding the Corona's in the air, I took another swig. The song changed (rapping'...) "Rock Bottom is the name of da click...Da airport to hot, so I'm hopping on the train with this brick."

She got up and tried to give me a lap dance.

She do have ass on her and I almost gave in, the beer is catching up to me at this point; either that or she slipped something In my bottle. I had to catch myself and remember why I was here. She was blocking my view from Tek and when I looked down I couldn't see him.

I pushed her out the way, got up and left. He wasn't at the bar or on the dance floor. "Damn, where the hell he go?"

As soon as I turned around I seen him walking to the bathroom and before I went in I pulled out my .45 with the silencer on it, and cocked back the four pound bar.

I cracked the door and through the mirror I can see Tek taking a leak. Somebody is next to him and by me not knowing what the guy looked like I walked in wit my pistol ready. Tek looked at me and signaled that the guy was in the last toilet stall. I went into the first one and closed the door, looking through the crack of the stall, I can see the other guy that was next to Tek leave.

Tek went to the middle stall and closed the door. Our target was in the last stall and sounded like a woman was in there with him. When I heard the toilet flush and the door open, we jumped out pointing the guns directly at his head. The woman started screaming and ran outta the bathroom.

"I know I'm da last nigga you wanna see right now. You thought I was dead huh?"

"Wait DON'T...!" Before he could get his last word...

" Schut!...fip..fip..fip!"

Tek put one in his head and he fell back into the stall, and I finished him off with three into his chest.

"Let's get outta here, Dawg!" we ran outta the bathroom and got outta the club quick.

"Damn did you see the look on that niggas face when he saw me?" Tek yelled and started laughing.

"Dawg, ole' girl looked like she shit in her pants. She took off like she was running the 100-meter dash." We started laughing again.

"Let's go get something to eat man; I don' worked up an appetite." Tek suggested.

We went to Nikki's across the street from Greek Town Casino and after we left, I figured we should stop at the strip club to check on Bamby.

It seems like everybody that left the State came straight here. It was cars everywhere.

"What's up B, how you doing?"

"I'm doing okay, how you?"

"I'm making it."

"You don't look to good. Are you okay?"

"Yeah I just got a lot of things on my mind that's all."

"Would you like a dance baby?"

Some chick came up to Tek trying to make some money. They left and went to the back somewhere.

"So, where is this clown you have been telling me about?"

"I don't know but he has been coming here a lot looking for you. You sure you don't know him?"

I couldn't tell 'cause he had his hat cocked real low."

"Well, he sure as hell know you."

Sitting here scoping out the club I can see and smell weed and booty in the air.

"Wait! That's him right there!" Bamby shouted and pointed to the back to the club.

"I'm 'bout to holla at this nigga."

"Hold on, he signaling to come there now."

"Well, go see what he wants then."

She walked over to his table and while they were talking she kept looking back at me, finally she walked back my way.

"What he want?"

"He wants you to come over to his table."

"Who the hell is this cat?"

"I don't know."

I walked over to the table and sat down. He took a sip out of his cup before looking up, still with his hat cocked down I couldn't see who this fool was. He took another sip and started to take of his hat. I see Tek coming toward the table. I guess Bamby told him what was up and where I was. As he was walking over to the table I see him with his hands on his pistol. I gave him a look telling him to back up for a second.

The man in front of me began taking off his hat, and I'm sitting here anticipating, waiting to see who the hell it was that has been looking for me.

By this time, I'm starting to grab my pistol under the table just to make sure nothing goes sour.

Finally, after everything seemed like it was slow motion, his hat was off and I could NOT believe who stood before my eyes!

It was my Damn Uncle!

"You surprised to see me huh?"

I'm sitting here lost for words.

"You thought I was gon' be gone forever? You see, one thing about me is that I always keep my word. You forgot that shit I told you before I went to prison? Naw... you couldn't have, cause you wouldn't be sitting here with that dumb ass look on your face!"

I began to build up so much anger that I just wanted to end this nigga right here, but too many people was around.

"Oh so what, you ain't got nothing to say lil nigga?"

By that time I couldn't take no more. I jumped over the table and slapped him with my pistol and ran toward the door.

"Glah!"

He fixed a shot off toward me, but he missed as I ran out the door. When I got outside Tek was in the truck waiting on me, and I jumped in.

"Dawg, did you get em?" Tek asked.

"Naw but the nigga just tried to shoot me!"

"Who?"

"My uncle!"

"Yo' uncle? When did he get out?"

"I don't know but he had to be out for a while cause I seen this nigga two weeks ago when I was here talking to Bamby."

"So what you gon' do?"

"I don't know what ima do but ima do it! If I gotta take this nigga out myself."

I went to Tek's house just so I could gather my thoughts on what I was gonna do about this situation. Everything didn't really register to me just yet, cause how the hell has Willie been going to see him and he's been out all this time? I definitely gotta figure some things out by the morning.

When Water Becomes Thicker Than Blood

Sherrad O'Neil Glosson

CHAPTER 13

When Bamby left the bar that night, my uncle Smitty followed her home. He managed to keep a nice distance from her so that she wouldn't recognize him and it worked all the way to her house. She got out the car and went to the trunk and grabbed her purse. Smitty was parked a block away but he had been watching her through binoculars the whole time.

When she went into the house, she turned on the shower and went into the bedroom to undress. She turned on some music (Musiq Soulchild playing) and jumped into the shower. By this time, Smitty had already made his way around the back of her house trying to figure out the best way to break in. The first window he checked happened to be unlocked, so he crept in and realized that water was running so she must have been in the shower.

He opened the window to her bedroom some more and dived in head first; he then stood in the closet and waited till she came out.

Moments later, she came out the shower with a towel wrapped around her into the bedroom. That's when he jumped out.

"Hello, Ms. Bamby!"

"How did you get in here?" she said with a panicked tone, looking for a way out.

"Aww, come on baby. You not happy to see me?"

"Please get out now. I'm calling the Police!"

He walked up on her and she backed into a corner with tears coming down her face.

"I just want to know where my nephew at that's all."

"I don't know where he went!"

He grabbed her wet hair and pulled it back.

"Now, you wouldn't be lying now would you?"

"I swear, I haven't talked to him since I left the club!"

"Now, listen to me, and listen to me carefully, when you talk to him, and you will talk to him soon; tell him that if he wants to see his precious little Bamby alive he needs to come and see me. You got that?"

"Yes!!" she screamed, fearfully.

He threw her head into the ground and left out the front door. Bamby ran to her phone immediately and called me.

"L.C. it-it's me!" she said sniffling."

"What's up B, What's wrong?"

"H-he was here!"

"WHO?"

"The guy from the club, he said if you ever want to see me alive, you need to come see him!"

"Are you okay?"

"Yes, I'm okay; can you please come over here?"

"I'll be there in a minute!"

When I got to Bamby's house, she was fully dressed and had her bat in her hand. She looked like she had been crying since we got off the phone. I embraced her.

"Are you okay?"

"I am now!"

"What exactly did he say?"

"He said, he wants you to contact him ASAP. What does he want with you?

"It's a long story B."

"Just tell me please!"

"Alright look…"

I sat down and told her the whole story about what was going on and by the time I was through, she had fallen asleep in my arms with the bat still in her hand. All night I stayed awake wondering if this nigga was going to come back. I can't believe he had the nerve to come at Bamby like that. All this time this nigga been out and my mom's husband acted like he ain't even know. I definitely gotta check into this and get it figured out. I need to make some kind of sense of this.

CHAPTER 14

I called up Lo and Tek and told them to meet me at Belle Isle. It was only two things for me to do at that time, which was to make sure I was safe, and most importantly that Bamby was straight.

Heading downtown I took Grandriver instead of the freeway to buy sometime to get my thoughts on track. I can't believe I almost shot my Damn uncle last night. I didn't think it was going to come to that point, but by him taking a shot at me, I know I can't hesitate anymore. The next time ima' have to go with my first mind instead of being indecisive. I know that nigga Willie has some explaining to do. I wonder if my mom knows anything about this. I wonder would she tell me though if she did.

Riding down Jefferson about two minutes from the Belle Isle bridge, I pulled into the Big Boys parking lot across the street from it and parked. I just wanted to come in after Lo and Tek did, so I waited until they arrived. Bamby was calling me, but I kept ignoring the call sending her text messages instead. I didn't want to talk at that moment, but I knew she was only worried about me. She was comfortable sleeping in my arms last night and I could tell cause' she only slobs in her sleep when she is with me. I guess she only feels protected when I am around. It's good that we still remain friends after we called the relationship off because most girls are cut off when it is over. Bamby was special to me though and I care about her as well.

I look up and see Tek on his bike going over the Belle Isle bridge and moments later Lo was on his bike right behind him. I started the car and proceeded right behind them.

"What's up, fella's?"

"What the fuck are you doing here?" Tek said with anger referring to Lo.

"Nigga, im here cause' Im here, Nigga what you got a problem?"

"Yeah, nigga the problem right here" Tek lifted up his shirt showing his pistol.

"Wait! Hold on ya'll niggas chill out. I told both of ya'll to meet me here for a reason." I stepped between both of them stretching me arms out to separate them.

Tek never liked Lo since the first day I introduced them. Tek said he had a fucked up vibe about him and just on that note he ever showed any concern for him. Even when they were in the joint, every time Tek said he didn't like

somebody because of their vibe, and as time went along,
Tek's premonition was right and we had to fuck many niggas
up. Lo was my cuz' so I couldn't let nothing happen to him,
even though we wasn't that close.

"I need to talk to ya'll for a minute. Obviously I got a
real big situation on my hands that I need to handle but don't
know how."

Both men gave me their undivided attention.

"I think it'll be best if I leave the country for a few
months to think for a while."

"Where you gon' go, Dawg?" Tek asked.

I answered as I looked across the Detroit River,
"Canada."

"Canada?" Both of the shouted simultaneously.
"What the hell you gon' go over there for?"

"I need to go somewhere that I know I can't easily be
tracked for a while. Now, ima keep ya'll niggas posted, and I
won't be gone long at all. Lo, I need you to go by the shop
periodically and make sure Auntie is running things
smoothly. Tek I need you to be my eyes and ears. Lo stop by
my crib every now and then and make sure everything is
okay and still in its place, as well as Bamby's spot. I got a
few people in Canada that I used to mess with back in the

day when I was in college playing ball. Give me about three months to get my thoughts together and I'll be back, alright?"

They both nodded in disbelieve and gave me dap, as we said our farewells. They hopped on their bikes and took off as I stayed and looked at Canada's view from across the water.

"Hello, B it's me. I need you to pack some of your things because we bout to take a long vacation."

"Where to?"

"I'll explain it when I get there, just be packed and I'll be there tonight alright?"

"Okay!"

We hung up the phone.

Then, I just cruised the streets of Detroit one more time before I departed.

At about 6:30 p.m., I stepped through the door. She had bags everywhere.

"Damn B, you wasn't playing were you?"

"You told me to pack because we were taking a LONG vacation."

"Yeah, but I didn't want you to pack up the whole living room!" I said laughing being sarcastic.

"Boy, shut up!"

I called a taxi and we headed out the door.

Because I had a felony I had to lay low. You can't cross the border to Canada with a felony or even while you are on probation. I just told the cab driver to take us across the border to Windsor and we would catch the plane.

When we arrived to the Exchange, I began to feel nervous because if they send me through customs and see all the baggage, they are going to ask a lot of questions, maybe even my real name.

"May I ask where you folks are headed to?" the exchange worker asked.

"Uh, we are going to the casino."

"How long are you going to be over here?"

"Uh… maybe about an hour or so." I replied. "Tryna get rich, and out quick, fast and in a hurry." I said smiling trying to convince her.

"How often do you come across the border?"

Damn, I wish this lady would stop asking us questions.

"Every three days or so I try my luck to win some money; I'm feeling like a million bucks tonight!"

She typed something in the computer and moments later… "Okay, you guys have a nice, safe night aye." We drove through the exchange and headed to the Windsor airport.

Driving, it takes about nineteen hours and two minutes to get to Manitoba, but on the plane it's about five hours. Once we got on the Windsor plane it was about a forty five minutes flight to Toronto; from Toronto to Ottawa it was about an hour and forty-five minutes, and then from Ottawa to Winnipeg it was about another hour and fifty minutes.

When we got off the flight at Winnipeg there was a Greyhound bus going to Brandon Manitoba which was about another two hour ride, so we grabbed some tickets and took off.

We arrived in Brandon, and went to this White boy's crib I used to run with when I was here. He didn't even know I was coming but hell, nobody did. It's nearly 1:00 am and every light in the house is on. When I got to the door it sounded like it was a damn after hour party going on. (Knock, Knock, Knock!) He didn't even bother to ask who it was; this nigga just opened the door.

"D-Town?" He just looked at me before realizing who I was. "D-Town! What's up, Buddy! How da? Who da? What da? What are you doing here? Come on in man!"

"What's up Hemings man. It's good to see you Homie."

"Man, where have you been Dawg?"

"Man, it's been rough over the past couple weeks I had to get outta the D for a minute."

"Well, you know you always welcome here, man. Who is this?"

"Oh, dis my home girl Bamby; I had to bring her with me you know."

"Yeah, it's all good. Damn, baby you single?" Hemings said jokingly.

"Man we just got here and you already trying to mack my girl!" I said laughing cause this White boy always knew how to ease weight of my shoulders.

"I'm just kiddin' man, ya'll come on in. Make yourselves at home! Me casa es su casa!"

"Dawg, you got a party going on? What ya'll doin' in the back?"

"Oh yeah just a couple of people from the Road House bar I invited over, you know how I do. Come and hang out with us, Bro!"

"Naw, man I think we gon' get some sleep. Good looking out my man!"

"Alright, no problem. You Fam!"

Hemings went back to his gathering and me and B went into the room to get situated.

"B, come here for a minute."

She came over and sat on the bed next to me.

"Now, I know this is a messy situation for you and I hate that things gotta be like this, but I promise you, you'll be safe. You believe me?"

She looked me in the eyes.

"Yes, I believe you."

We laid down and fell asleep in each other's arms.

I woke up to Hemings tapping my feet. He signaled me to follow him. I looked at the clock and I had only been sleep for a half an hour. Damn it seemed like I was asleep for hours. Bamby was knocked out, so I crawled outta the bed and walked into the living room, where I saw two females sitting on the couch.

"That's all for you bro, Welcome back!" Hemings said licking his lips. Looking at the two chicks had me horny in less than 3 seconds. I took my shirt off and set in between them.

"Hi?" one if the girls said shyly.

"How y'all doing tonight?"

"Awesome!" the white girls said at the same time pulling on my shorts. They could see the form of my dick poking through the shorts like I had a third leg.

"You not from around here are you?" they asked me.

"I'm familiar with the area."

One of the chicks started caressing my dick while the other one around my neck licking the inside of my ears. Next thing you know I'm getting some head, and looking at the hallway making sure Bamby don't wake up and go to the bathroom, cause she'd be pissed.

I laid down on my back and the chick that was giving me head switched positions and sat on my face, while the other chick began to suck me up like a popsicle. I felt like Hugh Hefner, but I was sober as hell so I knew I wasn't going to hold a nut.

"Hold on, let's get it popping!" I whispered.

I bent one of the girls over, and while she was licking her girls' pussy, I was putting my drill game down, pounding from the back.

"Aw!" she yelled

"Shhh... Be easy baby, don't yell!" I whispered to her.

I took one of my socks off my feet and put one in her mouth.

"Here bite on this!" As I continued to run up in her like I was racing against time. Slap..slap..slap..slap...slap

"DDDamn baby!" I whispered, as I nutted all on her back. I could tell that the other female was upset she couldn't get no dick and I kinda felt bad for her so three minutes later

I was ready to drill again. I bent her over as well and began to thrust away. She was eating the other girls' pussy from the back as I was making her ass clap.

"AW...AW... OUCH!!" She yelled. I smacked her ass.

"You gotta be quiet Dammit!" I took my other sock and put it in her mouth, and looked back down the hallway to make sure Bamby didn't hear.

"I gotta get this nut quick and get outta here!" I thought to myself.

"Um… um!" She moaned with the sock in her mouth, and I pulled out and skeeted all on her hair; I jumped up and ran to bathroom to clean up and went back to bed. Bamby was still asleep.

"Damn it feels good to be back in Canada." I said, smiling. I got back in the bed and passed out.

$$$

Meanwhile, back at home, Lo walked in his house, when he cut on the lights, Smitty was sitting there smoking a Newport.

"What's up, Nephew?" Lo jumped in shock.

"Unc, what the hell you doin' here?"

"I came here looking for you. What, you ain't happy to see yo' uncle?"

Lo walked over to him and gave him a hug. "Good to see you, Unc."

"Good to see you, Nephew."

"How da hell did you get out when you had a muthafuckin life sentence?"

"Aw, come on Nephew, just cause I went to the joint don't mean I'm dead. I still know people and I'm still da man around here."

Lo just stood there in shock cause he hadn't seen his uncle in so long. He went into the kitchen and got a couple of brews and came back and sat on the couch.

"Where Leon been at?"

Lo acted like he didn't hear him, just sat there listening to the radio.

"Oh so you didn't hear me talking to you?"

"Huh, what you say?"

"I said where yo' cousin at?"

"Uh... I don't know."

"Oh so you gone try to play me like I'm a stranger now?"

"He went outta town."

"Outta town where?" Smitty sat up to the edge of the chair.

"He went to Canada."

"CANADA? How da hell you let him go to Canada?"

"He said he was going for a few months."

"Is that right?" Smitty took a swig of his beer and sat back in the chair.

Lo couldn't believe he just ratted his own cousin out.

"Let me tell you something, Lo. I want you to get this real clear cause I'm only saying this one time and one time only." Smitty pulled out a .38 and set it on his lap. Lo jumped back looking at the gun.

"I wanna know all about his whereabouts, the hoes he be fuckin' wit, and everything else. I already got his bitch Maria on my team and you better get with the program too or you gon' have to pay a price yo' self and I know you don't want no problems. Do you?"

Lo just nodded his head and took another sip of his beer and closed his eyes.

"I'm expecting this information soon so you better get out in the streets now!"

Lo was still just sitting there. Smitty cocked his gun and Lo stood up like a toy soldier and walked out the door.

When Water Becomes Thicker Than Blood

\

CHAPTER 15

I woke up to the smell of some good ole Canadian bacon and some perogies. Bamby was tossing and turning all night because she couldn't sleep.

"What's up B? How you feel?"

"I'm doing okay."

I kissed her forehead and went to the bathroom to handle my business.

"What's up bro?" Hemings said as I came into the living room.

"What's good Homie? How was your night?"

He looked towards his room and so did I, looking at the two women who stayed overnight.

"Pretty good, Hemings, pretty good! Dig this though, Ima have to run to Winnipeg today to holla at Juan, Giddy, and Uddy. Bamby gon' stay here while I'm gone alright?"

"Alright bro, whatever you need. I gotchu' you."

I went into the room and told Baby what was going down, and to make sure she didn't have a problem with it. I got my things together and headed to the bus station for Winnipeg.

$$$

Doo Whop had another job offer for another hit for ten stacks. One of the local Detroit rap groups was beefing with each other and one of their homeboys got shot up with a .45. They needed Doo Whop to handle the shooter ASAP and as usual Doo Whop didn't have a problem doing it. Doo

Whop was real clever at what he did and unlike any hit man at his age that I ever knew.

He went to the Dickies Outlet across from the old Detroit Stadium on Trumbell and bought an all brown dickie shirt and pants with some brown boots to match. Where he had to go was not far from where he was at, so he drove close by the crib and parked around the corner. He went to the trunk of the car and pulled out a small box and walked around the corner to the house.

He walked up to the door and rung the door bell.

Ding…dong…

"Who is it." A woman answered.

Doo Whop was thrown off because only his target was supposed to be their alone. So he had to improvise. In which it wasn't a problem for him anyway.

"It's the UPS. You have a delivery."

"Oh, ok." She said opening the door in her robe.

"Is your husband home?"

"Oh he is not my husband, but he is upstairs taking a bath."

"Is that right."

Scutt….

Doo Whop shot her with the pistol he had in his hand under the box and before she could hit the ground Doo Whop caught her and laid her down easy. He wasn't expecting to do this much work, but just like the ole saying goes "When life throws you lemons, make lemonade." Of course that saying is universal.

He took her body and carried it to one of the rooms in the basement and ran back upstairs.

He looked up stairs to make sure his target was still there.

"Baybe" he yelled from upstairs." Doo Whop tiptoed up the stairs quick and smooth, as if he had feathers on his feet. He pushed the door open slowly and as usual it made that long squeaky noise.

"Bay, who is that at the door?"

Doo Whop came through the door and instantly put one in his head. He fell back into the wall and slid down into the bathtub. Doo Whop stood there and looked at him for a second admiring his work, then moments later he left and took off.

$$$

Uddy, Juan, and Giddy are my Homies I used to run wit when I was here playing ball. Them boys was getting money like crazy. When we were back in Brandon going to college, we used to come down to Winnipeg and party all night. Them Jamaicans be getting it in especially when Sean Paul or Bob Marley comes on.

"What up boys?" I said, coming through.

They were sitting on the couch rolling up some weed.

"D-Town? What's up Mo'n!! What's going on?"

"Nothing much. What's up wit ya'll?"

"Just sitting here rolling up a little Dutch you know. Sit down, Mo'n. What are you doing here?" Uddy said with his Jamaican accent.

I didn't bother to tell them what I was really here for. I just kept it simple as if I was just here for a vacation for real.

After smoking a few blunts and listening to Jamaican music all day and night it was time to go out to the club.

"I know you remember tis', Mo'n." Giddy pulled out a bottle of Jamaican rum.

The first time I drunk some of this I was too drunk. I think I even passed out a few times, although it tasted like medicine, you sho'll be lit for the whole night. When he pulled that out I knew what kinda night it was gon' be.

"It used to have you hurling all over the place, Mo'n and sleeping like a lil baby!"

We all busted out laughing thinking about how we used to get smashed in college.

They poured me a cup and put some milk in it as usual. When I took the first sip, it sparked so many memories; I just downed it with one swallow.

"Aw yea Mo'n. You back now!"

We all drunk about four cups before we headed to this club called Beach.

We got to the club and it's people everywhere. When we step out all eyes be on us. All four of us were pretty nice size and me with my swagger and American slang all the ladies bowed down to me.

"Can I buy you a drink?", this caramel complex woman asked me with a French Canadian accent.

"Naw, that's alright, baby girl, but I do want you to save me a dance later on, alright."

She nodded her head and smiled as we went to the table and posted up.

"Shake Dat Ting", a song by Sean Paul, came on and the dance floor became crowed.

The liquor was in me something heavy. I couldn't stay seated for too long so I hit the dance floor and started doing my one –two step, drunk as all out doors.

I was starting to get back used to how things were before I left and went back to Detroit. Females left and right were coming to dance with me all at the same time. I was feeling like Diddy!

Me, Giddy, Uddy, and Juan was stealing the spotlight from every guy in there. It's so crowded and hot that it felt like sweat kept flying everywhere. We didn't think nothing of it though at the time.

"Uddy, did you feel that?"

"Yeah, Mo'n. What was it?"

"I don't know?"

I looked around the club and looked up noticing some white guys with army clothes on standing above our heads with beers in their hands.

"Aye, Uddy, I think them fools up there throwing beers on us."

We both looked up and they acted like nothing was happening. We kept dancing doing our one-two thing then we felt another drop. This time Juan and Giddy felt it too. They looked straight up and the army dudes we laughing. Giddy is so pissed he shot up the stairs as fast as he could and we were all behind him.

When we got up the stairs it had to be about twelve of them, but we didn't care. I know I didn't and if they really knew how I got down they'll be kissing my shoes right now. They was looking like they were ready to get some cash and I was ready to draw my pistol, but I realize I didn't bring one across the border. "Dammit" I love looking at niggas faces when that pistol is in play. We all had problems before in clubs, whereas niggas was haten' and we had to turn over a few tables, so this wasn't anything new. But the look on Giddy's face, I knew it was about to go down. I took my Cartier's off and put'em in my pocket and turned my hat backwards.

"Aye, what's ya problem, Mo'n?" Giddy walked up into he guys face.

Two of the bouncers came outta nowhere and tackled the two who was throwing beer at us; they must have been watching the play the whole time.

The bouncers always made sure we were straight; for one, we all went to the same school together, and for two, we always spend big at the bar.

After that situation, the bouncer kicked the army dudes out and a song by Beanie Man came on. Giddy went back to feeling like doing his one-two step and we all went back to the dance floor.

"Yo, D-Town, control your tings!" Juan hollered out while I had three women trying to grind on me.

"I heard you Dawg. I got em!"

We danced the night out and by the time we left we were still revved up.

"Aye Mo'n. Lets hit tis' afta pahty yo!" Giddy suggested.

We all agreed and headed to the Jamaican spot down town. We were a little starved by that time so we left and went and got some curry chicken on the way.

When we got into the club it was nothing but Jamaicans and Nigerians everywhere. It was only one light on in there and that was at the DJ booth.

As soon as we hit the door, we went straight to the dance floor.

Wayne Wonder was coming through the speakers, "No letting go, no holding back…" We hit the floor hard, not even missing a beat.

As I was dancing, I noticed this female I used to mess with back in the day.

"What's up, Grace? How you doing?"

"D-Town!! How ya been, Mo'n?"

"I've been alright. Girl, look at you!"

She was about five foot seven, one hundred sixty pounds, with more curves than a hour glass. I twirled her around checking out her figure.

"So, what's up, Mo'n? You're back for good tis' time?"

"Naw, I'm just here on vacation that's all."

'What you doing tonight?" she asked.

"It's already 3:30 and you trying to do something right now?"

"If you're not busy, I am!"

In my mind all I'm thinking about is Bamby, wondering how she's doing in Brandon with my boy, Hemings.

"Well, I am kinda busy, but gimmie your number and I'll hit you up alright!"

"Okay, not tah problem!", she replied with a sad look on her face, as she turned and walked away.

I'm tryna figure out why da hell I'm thinking about Bamby when I got women throwing themselves at me all night.

After we left the after hour joint we went back to the gates.

"Awl, Mo'n D-Town, I'm so glad you back Mo'n!" Uddy hollered out.

"Yeah, it's good to be back, Dawg."

"So, what made you come just out the blue?"

"Man, it was a lot of situations that have occurred over the last few weeks that I had to leave for a minute, you know, but it's all good though."

"You remember that guy that we were beefing with before you left?"

"Uh... Yeah, Biggs right?"

"Yeah, we got a little problem with him too, and tomorrow it's going to be a big hit. You down?"

I knew it was too good to be true. I walked away from one problem and walked into another one. Biggs was one of the drug dealers I had a problem with back when I was here years ago. He knew I was moving some weight from here back to the city, and he didn't like the fact that I didn't need his assistance. Typical type of hatin' ass niggas of course. They everywhere. I wanted to kill his ass then anyway.

"Yeah, you know I'm down if you need me."

"Alright then, tomorrow it's on."

I went in the back room drained, as soon as I hit the pillow I fell right asleep.
I felt like I was being shaken and when I realized what was going on I couldn't believe it.

"What the hell are you doing here?"

"Let me tell you once again baby boy. I know people. You thought I wasn't going to find you just because you came to Canada. Ha! I'm glad you thought so."

I backed up into the top of the bed, thinking how I was going to get out of this one. "Where in the hell is Uddy, Giddy and Juan, I thought and how the hell did he get in here?'

"Oh, and for the record, don't worry about them lil niggas that was in the front room. I took care of them easily. They singing hymns to God in heaven right now." He said smiling.

I reached for my gun but realized I didn't have it on me.

"Fuck!" I said to myself.

He just sat in the chair by the door calmly looking at me while I was trying to figure out how I was going to make my next move. He pulled out a 9mm and cocked it back.

"Well, nephew, I guess this is where we leave off huh? What you think about dat?"

I just looked him in the eyes and then at the barrel; back at his eyes then back at the barrel.

"Blayah!!"

I jumped up covered with sweat. I didn't know what time it was but it felt like been sleep for hours. I still had my clothes on from the club, and my head was banging like crazy.

"3:30 pm?" I said looking at my cell phone.

"Naw, Mo'n it's 2:30 pm. Your back in Canada, Mo'n!"

"Oh, yeah. I forgot."

I called Hemings' crib to see what was up with Bamby.

"What's up Hemings?"

What's up, Bro? what's going on?"

"Awl, man, you know it was a crazy night. Where's Bamby?"

Moments later she came to the phone.

"Hello?'

"What's up B, how you doing?"

"I'm doing better now that I am talking to you."

"That's good. I'll be back up there some time tonight, probably around eight."

"Okay, I'll be waiting on you as usual."

I busted out laughing, "Girl, you silly. I'll see you later!"

We hung up the phone and I went into the living room where Uddy and Juan were sitting on the couch listening to Timbaland and Magoo. Sitting at the computer was Giddy, rolling up a Dutch.

"What's up, Mo'n? I see you're alive?"

"Yeah, it was a long night for me!"

What happened to dat ting from da afta pahty?" Giddy asked.

"I sent her on her way. I got her number though, so it's still always a go, you know. Ain't nothing changed, Homie! I'm still the big man on campus!"

They started laughing, as they began to pass the blunt and talk about last night's episodes.

I took a couple of puffs and went into the back room to call my homeboy, Tek.

"What's up, Baby?"

"What up doe, Homie? What's hood?"

"Shit. What's going on down there?"

"Awl man, yo cousin, he been on some real slime ball shit, ya know. I gotta keep a real good eye on him Dawg for real."

"Is that right?"

"Yeah, Dawg, I keep that nigga close just so I can keep a closer look on his movements."

"Yeah, Man, keep doing that. I know that's my cousin and all, but if that nigga get outta line…"

"I hear you. Homie, but what's going up there though?"

"Just catching up on old times so far. I got a little situation ima take care of tonight, but other than that it ain't nothing too much I can't handle. Ya dig?"

"Yeah, I hear you, but what's up with Shorty? She good?"

"Yeah, she straight, I got her chilling at one of my home boy's cribs up in Brandon."

"Oh, that's cool, but listen... if you need, me, just let me know, alright?"

"I hear you, Dawg. Just keep an eye on Cuz for me alright?"

"Enough said, Son. I got you!"

We hung up the phone and all I could think about it is my cousin on some bullshit, and I might have to go back home a little sooner than I expected.

Nighttime rolled around and it was time to take care of some business.

"Yo, what's up Mo'n, you ready to ride?"

"Let's get it!"

We hopped in the car and headed to our destination. Listening to 50 Cent, "Get rich or die trying" This album had me ready for war. ... (Song playing) "Many men, wish death on me, blood in my eye Dawg and I can't see, I'm trying to be what I'm destined to be, but niggas trying take my life away. Many men..." I was thinkin' about back home; my uncle tryna get at me and my emotions went straight in rage mode.

"Aye, man, where da pistols at?"

"Oh, right here, Mo'n!", Juan shouted pulling at .25 and handing it to me."

"Dawg, what da hell am I gon' do with dat, put water in it and squirt?"

We all started laughing.

"Man, get me a real gun, please."

"Okay, Mo'n, I got you right here!"

He pulled out a Tech 9.

"Oh, yeah baby, that's what I'm talking about right there. Now, we cookin' with grease!"

We pulled up to this mansion estate. Giddy gave me the orders and I followed them through. Uddy walked around back and cut off the lights. We kicked the front door in and searched for our target. I went to the left while Juan went straight and Giddy went to the right. I hear someone yelling upstairs.

"Who da hell messing wit me lights, Mo'n?"

Apparently, it had to be somebody else in the house, and with a crib like this; it gotta be more than one.

I went through the dining room toward the kitchen area leading to the steps.

"Who tryna mess wit ta big Mo'n yo?" He shouts out.

I could tell by the echo of the walls that his room was clear to the stairwell, and I didn't know where everybody else went, but I started tip toeing up the stairs slowly with my gun pointed in front of me. I got the infra red beam straight ahead.

As I got to the front of the stairs I'm waiting on Biggs, pointing the tech for him to say another word. By that time Juan, Giddy, and Uddy was coming up the stairs and I signaled them to be quiet.

"Who's there?" Biggs yelled out from behind me.

I whispered to Juan, "On the count of three we going in."

"3!"

I burst through the door and ducked off to the left.

"Bloom!" "Bloom!" "Bloom!"

All I heard was a shotgun let out a couple rounds and Juan fell to the floor.

"Doof!" "Doof!" "Doof!" "Doof!" "Doof!" "Doof!'

Immediately, I let out a few catching him right in the left eye.

"Juan, you alright?" I hollered out.

"He shot me yo; I can't feel my legs, Mo'n!"

I went over to check on him and he said he couldn't walk. I put him on my shoulder and as I was walking out the room, we had more company.

A little kid who looked like he had to be about fourteen had a pistol in his hand. I jumped back in the room and told Giddy without even hesitating.

"Giddy and Uddy get in front of me and lead the way!"

Giddy ran in the hallway… "Pow!" "Pow!" "Pow!"

He knocked the lil kid off his feet and back down the steps.

We ran down the stairs to more company.

"Uddy DUCK!!"

"Doof!" "Doof!" "Doof!" "Doof!"

I took two of the dudes who looked like they were his body guards out with four shots, with Juan still on my shoulder.

"Hold on man. You gon' make it. We almost there!!"

"I'm starting to see the light, Mo'n!"

I could tell by the sound of his voice, that he was going unconscious.

"JUAN!!!" I hollered, while running to the front door. "Juan, you alright, man?"

By that time, he had become silent.

I took him off my shoulder and laid him on the grass, checking his pulse, realizing he was gone.

We just left him and drove off.

Sitting in the back seat listening to Giddy and Uddy cry about the hit going wrong, all I could think about is, I don' came at the wrong time. I tried to step away from a problem, but walked into another and lost a homie in the process. I guess that's why they say, you shouldn't walk away from your fears, you should walk towards them. We arrived back at the gates and I cleaned myself up and headed back to Brandon.

When Water Becomes Thicker Than Blood

CHAPTER 17

When I got back to Hemmings', Bamby was the only one up in the house sitting on the couch.

"B, what's up?"

"Hey!"

"Why you sittin' in the dark?"

"I was missing and worried about you!"

I was just quiet for a minute because I really didn't know that this girl still cared about me this much. I mean I knew she still wanted to get back with me, but I didn't know her feelings were still so strong.

I took my shirt off and sat next to her on the couch.

"You miss me, huh?"

She nodded her head, placing her hand on my chest as I wrapped my arms around her. I kissed her forehead and she looked at me. While starring at her, I could feel some emotion and after everything I just went through in Winnipeg, I was in need of some affection. I could tell she was feeling me the same way so I kissed her on her lips gently and she started kissing me back.

She began to kiss me on my chest, and started licking my stomach. She laid me back and climbed on top and she began to kiss my neck. Feeling this deep, sexual chemistry; I started pulling her shirt over her head. Looking into her eyes and then at her sexy body (something I hadn't seen in a long time), starring at her made me want her even more.

I unsnapped her bra and laid her softly on her back as I began to kiss and lick her belly button. She began to moan in ecstasy as I pulled off her booty shorts that she made from my sweat pants.

She didn't have any panties on and her girl was so juicy, warm, and moist. She shaved just like I like.

I started kissing her feet, sucking her toes, and making my way up to her legs. By the time I worked up to her thighs, her body began to quiver. Her legs were already shakin' and I hadn't even went to work yet.

I began to lick inches away from her precious gates, teasing her. I pulled out my manhood and turned her over on her stomach. We laid across the arm of the couch and I inserted my 8 inch piece inside her soul.

"Ooh, Baby!", she moaned as I took my time, making sure I hit every spot. The G-Spot, L, M, and P spots of her insides.

"Sh-Shiitt! Just like that.. Oh Shhitt! I miss this s-so much!", she said muttering.

I grabbed her by her pony-tail, pulled it back and began to fuck her. Pounding her ass as hard as I could, I pulled out, made her wait, and slid my way right back in.

Pulling her hair, I was giving her the ride of a lifetime. She began to throw it back.

"D...do-do-Don't Sto-Stop! I-I-I'M!!"

I was hitting it so hard, she couldn't even get her words out.

"Ooh-ooh, ohh! I-I-I'mm cum-cummin'!!!"

She came all over my piece.

As I pulled it out, her cream was all over my shaft! She turned around and began to lick it off.

As she was giving me pleasure, she began to use her hands, massaging my man. Serving me like a pro, my eyes were in the back of my head. I was going crazy!

"Damn Baby, you serving me right!"

She straddled me in the reverse cowgirl position and grabbed my ankles and started bouncing on my shaft like she was riding a horse, as if it was the last time she would ever get the chance to do so.

Looking at her ass from the back bouncing up and down, I couldn't help but to cum.

Seconds later, all over her back; I squirted my love on her.

All of a sudden I look up and see Hemmings in the kitchen with his mouth wide open and a cup in his hand. Bamby noticed him too, but didn't care. She wanted to show how she pleased her man, or ex-man, I suppose.

"Hemings, what da hell you doing?"

He just stood there nodding, with his mouth still open.

Bamby got up and headed to the shower and I followed her.

"L.C., wake up!", Bamby shook me.

"Huh?"

"Wake up; it's somebody at the door."

I looked at the clock and it read 7:36 a.m. I wonder who the hell this could be this time of morning. Hemmings must've heard the door at the same time cause I see him staggering outta his room putting his glasses on.

"Who the hell you got coming over?"

"I don't know, man."

"Who is it?" Hemmings yelled walking to the front door.

"Detroit Free Press!"

I walked back into the room and laid back down once I heard it was the Detroit Free Press newspaper.

"Wait the Detroit Free Press?" I thought.

"BLAYAH!"

"What da hell?"

I jumped back outta da bed and ran back into the living room only to see Hemmings lying on the floor with his chest blown off, shaking.

I ran to the front door and didn't see nobody.

"Hemmings can you hear me? Talk to me!"

He was coughing up so much blood he could barely breathe.

"What the!"

"B,... go back in the room please!" I shouted.

I can't call the police because I'm a felon and if I get caught, they can give me two years in prison over here.

"B, pack up! We outta here!"

"What we gon' do wit him?"

"Ima take care of it. Just pack up!"

I called in a report that I heard a shooting at a house nearby. Me and Bamby fled the scene.

I had enough money in the bank so we went to this hotel next to this bar called Houston's.

"Leon, I'm scared, I can't deal with this anymore!"

"You trust me right?" She nodded her head "yeah".

"Alright then, when the time is right we gon' head back to Detroit, but I gotta think things through before I go back you hear me?"

She nodded her head again. I kissed her on the forehead and laid down in the bed with her next to me as she fell asleep. I just stayed there thinking about how everything that has been taking place. I got 99 problems and a bitch ain't one for real.

Thinking about what my granddad was saying a while ago was starting to register in my head again. I did something I haven't done in years. I got down on my knees and prayed.

$$$

Smitty had caught up to Lo again while he was at the shop talking to Andell. Lo was a lil' scared knowing that his uncle was on some bullshit. That's what happens when you get a nigga to fear you. You have him doing what ever you want him to do and that's exactly how Smitty had Lo.

Smitty walked in the shop and Lo was sitting next to Andell while she was doing some hair.

"What's up Andell?" Smitty said coming through the door.

"Hey Smitty, boy you looking good. When you get out? What took you so long to come and see me?"

"I haven't been out too long. You know they can't keep a real O.G. down fo' ever."

"I hear that."

"Whats up Lo?"

"Whats up unc."

"Shit you tell me?"

"I'm on it."

"You on it huh? What the hell is that suppose to mean?" he walked up to Lo standing over him while he was still sitting down.

Andell was trying to be nosey and do hair at the same time. Lo didn't bother telling her what was going on. In fact, he didn't tell anybody. He was too scared that Smitty would find out.

"I'm on it a'ight." Lo replied.

"Yeah, ok."

"What ya'll talking about?" Andell asked.

"Lil Lo right here taking care of some business for me and he better move fast right down to modern time before his time run out. Literally."

Smitty pulled out a Newport and lit it taking a long pull, blowing the smoke in Lo's face. "Ash to ash, dust to dust" Smitty dumped ashes in Lo's lap. All that tough shit Lo used to be on was in check when Smitty was around and Smitty knew it. It was something about Smitty that made niggas get outta his way when he moved. Now that he don' spent years and years in the joint lifting weights he was like a tank coming through. He never wore a t-shirt and he barely wore wife beaters. You know how niggas act when they get outta prison.

"Well, look. I'm bout' to head over to All-stars and look at some ass real quick, Imma catch up with ya'll later a'ight." Smitty said walking toward the door.

"A Lo." He shouted with the cigarette still in his mouth." Right down to modern time lil nigga. The hour glass won't last long. Trust me."

$$\$\$\$$$

For about a month I stayed low in the hotel, just me and Bamby. I tried to stay low key for as long as possible. Looking at the news they didn't have any suspects in the murders in Winnipeg or on Hemings being killed and I didn't want to look suspicious to any of these Canadians. I already look like I'm not supposed to be around here, so at night is when I made most of my moves.

I haven't called Tek in a minute come to think of it, and my cousin, Lo, hadn't called me at all. I wonder what that was all about.

"Tek, what's up boy?"

"What up doe Homie? What's hood?"

"Nothing new, man, just chillin'. What's going on with you?"

"Man, it's been a lot of bullshit happening in the D man, straight up! Oh and yo cousin… I don't trust that nigga at all, Dawg! I think you need to holla at him for real. I swear if he wasn't yo cousin I would have to put a bullet in him, a long time ago."

"Is that right?"

"Yeah, he been hangin' wit yo uncle real tough lately too!"

"Oh yeah? Aye Homie, I'm about to try and call him, Ima hit you up in a min!"

We hung up the phone and I called Lo.

"Leave it!"

Damn it went straight to voicemail. I tried again...
"Leave it!"

I hung up the phone, not even leavin' no message. I hadn't called my mom since I been gone and I know she worried to death about me.

"LEON!" she answered in the first ring.

"What's up, Ma? How you doing?"

"Leon, where are you?"

"I'm not far, momma. Why you sound like something wrong?"

"Leon, they gonna kill you!"

"Who ma?"

"I heard Willie, Smitty, and Lo talking in the basement a few weeks ago and they were saying how they were gonna take care of you whenever you come back from Canada!"

I'm thinkin to myself, how the hell do they know where I'm at? Oh yeah, I told Tek and Lo before I left when we were at Belle Isle.

"I heard them asking Lo where in Canada you were, but he didn't know. He just told them you'll be back in a few months.

"Look, Ma, stop cryin'. Ima be alright! Okay?"

"Why do they want you dead Leon? What did you do?"

"It's a long story, Ma. I can't explain, but listen to me... Ima be back soon okay?"

"Okay, Leon, but please be safe okay?"

"Alright, Mama, talk to you later!" I hung up the phone thinking to myself, my own cousin turned his damn back on me. I mean I done had this nigga back from Day One. Now, I see what Tek was talking about.

"What's up, Homie? You were right about Lo, Dawg. I just talked to my mom and she told me some of the same stuff you been seeing in him."

"What you gon' do Dawg?"

"It's only one thing left to do, Homie!"

"Enuff said. I'll be waiting on you alright?"

We hung up the phone and I went back in the room to holla at Bamby. She was sitting in the chair looking out the window. I sat right next to her and grabbed her by the hand.

"B it's some things I gotta take care of back at home alright? Ima leave you here for a while, so I can go handle some business alright?"

"I don't wanna be here by myself, Leon!"

"I understand that, B. I really do, but I want you to be safe. You told me you trust me right?" She nodded her head "yeah".

"Alright, well tonight I'm heading back to the D and ima send for you in a minute okay?"

She stood up and sat on my lap, and kissed me on the lips.

"Make sure you send for me, okay?"

I got up, packed my things and headed out the door to the Greyhound bus station. When I got to the airport in Winnipeg, I had to go through United States customs again.

"Can I see you ID please sir?"

I gave the officer my ID and he kept looking at me with this strange look on his face.

"Where are you from?" , the black man asked.

"I'm from Detroit."

"Detroit, Michigan huh?"

I nodded my head avoiding eye contact. I knew what he was about to ask me next.

"What you doing all the way up here?"

"I play basketball up here for Brandon University."

"Is that right?" I nodded. "Well basketball season isn't over why are you leaving so early?"

"My mom is sick and I need to hurry home to make sure she's alright."

He remained silent for a second and I stayed looking everywhere else besides him.

"Okay, have a nice flight, and I hope your mom feels better!"

"Thanks!"

I got on the airplane and headed back to Detroit.

When I got back to the D, it was about 12:30 a.m. I rode by the shop to see how everything was looking. I see my auntie didn't do a real good job at keepin' it up and I had mail stacked to the top ceiling. One envelope stood out to me though, that didn't have a name on it. I opened it and looked inside to see pictures of me and my whereabouts around the city, pictures of my crib, with me coming out, me heading inside the bar where Bamby works, and pictures of me at

Becky's house. I thought nothing of it at first, but it was kinda strange.

I'm sitting here thinking who the hell could be possibly worried about where I'm at and what I'm doing; all they had to do was call. Then it hit me. Tek did tell me about my cousin and his actions. This nigga been setting me up the whole time. How else would my uncle know about me being at the bar and where I lived? Come to think of it, that day when I went home and noticed my windows were left open, he must've been there. Well, if he got pictures of me at Becky's spot then that means...

Despite the time, I called up Becky's crib to see if what I was thinking had any truth to it. She didn't answer the phone the first time, so I tried again. Still no answer so I left a message.

"Hey Becky, it's me--."

"So you made it back huh, Little Nigga? I thought you'll see it my way."

"Who da hell is this?"

"You know exactly who it is, Nephew. What you thought this was a game? I hold the truth to all my promises, you know that right, but just in case you didn't, let me remind you again."

I can hear Becky through the phone crying. It sounded like he had his hands over her mouth and she was trying to scream.

"If you lay a single hand on her, I swear!"

"Wait hold on, Nephew. I'm the one giving the orders around here. Just know that you can be touched and will be touched at anytime."

He hung up the phone and I immediately called up Tek.

"Tek, what's up, Homie?"

"What's up man? What's hood?

"I'm back in town and I don't know how my uncle knew already."

"How the hell he know dat?"

"I don't know man, but I think ima have to holla at him for real you know?"

"I told you, Dawg. Yo' cousin is on some folly.'

"Yeah, I hear you, but ima deal with him later. I'm on my way to pick you up now, alright!"

"A'ight!"

We hung up the phone and I sat down at my desk gathering my thoughts, but hell, I did enough thinkin when I was in Canada. I left the shop and went to Tek's house.

When I got there, he was standing on the porch smoking a cigarette.

"What's up, Dawggie?"

"You tell me!"

"You ready to take care of this, or what?"

"I guess its the only way, Homie."

He got into the car and we drove to Becky crib.

Becky stayed in Southfield on 10 mile and Lasher, and when we pulled up to her spot, it was pitched black, not a single light on in the whole house.

I walked up to the door and looked through the windows and couldn't see a thing. I called her phone and she picked up on the first ring.

"Leon!"

"What's up, I'm at the door!"

When she came to the door, she had a club in her hand crying.

"You alright?"

"I was sleeping in my bed until I heard the window bust. I woke up and went to the back door. He grabbed me around my neck and put his hands on my mouth. That's when you called. He said that it's your turn to come looking for him now!"

I embraced her and ensured her, she was safe.

We went back to the car, and told Tek what was up.

"Well, let's ride out and play this cat and mouse game!" Tek responded.

I hopped in the car and went in search of my Uncle Smitty. I called Lo up but he didn't answer the phone.

"Oh, so dat nigga actin' brand new now, huh?"

"I told you. You need to handle that!" Tek responded.

When Water Becomes Thicker Than Blood

CHAPTER 19

It's 4:39 a.m. and we've been riding around Detroit all night in search of my uncle Smitty. Now all of a sudden, he's nowhere to be found. That's alright though cause when I do find him; it's going to be hell to pay.

I'm a lil' hungry so me and Tek stopped at the Hollywood Coney Island on Grand River and Evergreen.

"You feel like going inside?" I asked.

"Naw man, let's just go through the drive-thru and go to my crib."

We both ordered some breakfast because it ain't nothing like Coney Island breakfast in the middle of the night. We got our food and headed The Notorious Exit 9 off the Southfield free-way to Tek's crib over on Joy Road and Southfield.

When we got there, we just sat on the porch, smoking a blunt and chilled listening to Young Jeezy's CD the "Recession". I was so heated and in kill mode that I couldn't go to sleep if I wanted to. I mean my cousin on some fake shit and my step father phony as hell. Maria talking about ima get mine sooner rather than later and my damn uncle got me playing his Tom and Jerry "catch me if you can game."

The blunt seemed like it lasted till the sun came up or maybe it just burned slow because we put honey on it. Tek has been quiet for some time now and I just now noticed.

"Aye man, wake up!" I shoved him.

"Huh... What?"

"Wake up fool!" I yelled. He was asleep with his mouth wide open.

"Aye look, Homie. It's 6:58 a.m. I need to go and check on a few things. Ima get at you later alright?"

"Alright man, get at me if you need me!" he said.

We gave each other five, and a half shoulder hug, and I hopped in the rental that I got from the airport.

My body is drained from the flight cause I still haven't laid down. I got jet lag, my eyes red as hell, and the only thing that was keeping me up at this point is the fact that I could be blindsided at any time.

I headed to my crib first to check on some things. I haven't been there in a couple of months. From the outside things looked good, but once I got closer to the door step things began to look a lil' suspect.

I opened the door and I could tell that somebody had been there. I looked around and when I looked down, there is foot prints on the carpet. I kneeled down and felt the print, and it was fresh. I know it can't be somebody here now, but you never know. I pulled a pistol I took from Tek and followed the foot prints; tip toeing through the living room, then though the kitchen, the prints led me to the basement.

I walked down the stairs and once I got to the bottom the prints disappeared. I looked around to see if everything was where it was suppose to be, and everything was good.

"Wait, hold on a second", I told myself.

I went to the safe where I kept my guns and money, it was completely empty.

"Damn! This nigga don' took all my guns, not only that, but he gon' try to use them against me?"

I ran back up stairs to check on my other stash. I went into the bathroom. Thank God it wasn't hit. I guess I was smart to hide one under my toilet. My phone started ringing and it scared the hell outta me. It was Bamby calling. I didn't wanna answer it but I did anyway.

"Hello!"

"Leon, it's me!" she said with a sad voice.

"B, what's up?

"I'm worried about you, Leon. Are you okay?"

For a second, I was quiet but I'm in killer mode and Bamby on the phone with this soft shit. I hope she ain't tryna say what I think she gon' say.

"B, I'm alright, I told you that Ima send for you alright!"

"I know you told me that but--"

"B, it's no but..."

"Okay, okay, I'll be here waiting for you, alright!"

"Alright, no doubt!"

"Leon?", when she said my name I already knew what was next.

"B, I gotta go!"

I quickly ended the phone conversation, and hung up the phone. I was ready to walk out the bathroom, until I heard a noise in my living room, It sounded like somebody was coming through the front door. I stayed still in the bathroom and cracked the door a little bit. I cut off the lights and stayed low.

I got mirrors everywhere in the living room so I can see pretty good. The noise stopped, I copped out the pistol. I tiptoed out the bathroom and through the hallway, towards where I heard the noise, then it started again. I can feel that I was close to whoever was in here because I can feel body heat. I always had good senses.

I got closer to the end of the hallway almost into the living room, and I can see the reflection off the blinds. I tiptoed again, another step. I'm thinking that it's gotta be my uncle, and I'm not about to waste no time in blowing his head right out.

"Who the hell is this?" I said to myself, and without hesitating I turned the corner and drew my gun.

Holding my pistol at this stranger's head, he rose up and looked at me.

"Dawg, what the hell are you doing here?" It was my cousin, Lo. He took a deep swallow because I was seconds away from blowing his brains all over my wall.

"What da hell you creeping for?" I asked. "You almost got yo' head blew off." I still had the gun pointed at his head.

"Man, I thought somebody was breaking into yo' spot. I saw a car parked in front of the driveway, and I knew it wasn't yours."

I took the pistol away from his head, but I still had it in my hand cocked back, and ready to blast off.

"Boy, what made you come here in the first place? Naw, wait! Never mind that, what's been going on since I've been gone?" I looked him in the eyes.

"Man, I don't know what you talking about. What somebody been telling you something?" He looked away.

"Naw man, you know what don't even worry about it. It's good to see you man."

I put my arms around him because he knew I knew he's been fucking up. I could see in him the very things Tek was telling me. I never really was close to him like that anyway, and I should just blast him right now but Ima make sure I get to the bottom off things before the night is over.

"Well, listen man; I gotta go take care of a few things so ima get at you later on." I said

"A'ight, well make sure, so we can hang out or something," he said walking out the door.

"Aye, Lo!" I shouted

"What's up?", he turned around

"Ima get at you for real, aight?" I said waving the gun pointing it at him.

He just kept walking without even saying another word.

I got some of my things together and left out to go to my shop.

Once I got there, it was looking like a damn spot house. I must have been so tired to even notice last night.

When I walked in my auntie wasn't even there.

"What's up Mika? Where Andell at?"

"I don't know. She said she was… here she come right now!" She pointed to the door.

"Hey, Nephew, what you doing here?", she said coming to the door eating some pig skins, smoking a Newport 100, with a Grape Faygo in the other hand.

"I own this shop, you forgot, and Auntie please put that out! Is this what's been goin' on since I been gone?" I asked looking at everybody that was there.

They all remained silent looking around at the next person to see who was going to say something first.

"Andell, let me holla at you in the back!" I motioned her to the back office.

She came in right behind me and sat on the couch still smoking and eating them pig skins. I sat on the top of my desk.

"What's been going on since I left?'

"Wh... I don't know... Like what?"

"Like anything. I've been gone for a couple of months and you gon' tell me that everything is everything? What's up with Smitty?", I asked her, and she got silent not even chewing.

"What have you heard?"

"You know exactly what I heard I--" My phone started to ring.

"Who the hell is this calling me unavailable?" I wasn't about to answer, but it could have been Bamby calling from a pay phone.

"Hello?" I yelled, all I heard was sniffling on the other end.

"Hello?" I yelled again.

"Leon, it-it's me."

"Ma? What's wrong? I stood up.

"My husband!"

"Yo husband what, Ma? Talk to me?"

"He b-ba-beat me!"

"WHAT!!" I shouted!

She started coughing

"Where are you ma?

"I'm in the hospital!"

"I'm on my way ma!" I hung up the phone and ran out the door.

CHAPTER 20

Once I got to the hospital I didn't even bother parking. I just pulled up to the front door and ran inside. I found my mother's room and walked in. I looked at her face and it looked like she had a black eye. She had fallen asleep, since we had gotten off the phone, and I kissed her on the forehead, and she woke up.

"Ma, are you okay?" I asked, rubbing her head

"Yeah baby, I'm doing fine I--", she started coughing. I'll be okay son!"

I'm standing here looking at her and she has bruises all on her arms.

"Why did he do this to you, Ma?"

"He heard me telling you about them trying to kill you when you came back. He started choking me and hitting me in the face."

Looking at her, and hearing her talk; it seemed like it was a normal thing for him to do.

"Ma, you are going to be alright. You hear me? Ima' take care of this situation alright!"

"Naw, baby. Just leave it alone, okay?"

"Leave it alone! Ma, he hurt you and it ain't no tellin' how long this has been going on!" A tear came down my cheeks. Now I am going to get to the bottom of this okay?"

"Okay, baby. Just be careful, okay!"

"Ma, ima be alright, okay. Don't worry about me. You just worry about you getting yourself better."

I looked her in the eye, and another tear came running down. I kissed her on the check and began to walk out the door.

"Leon!" she yelled as I was halfway out. I turned around. Be careful!"

I nodded my head and right then and there I knew what time it was. When I got outside the hospital, I called Lo.

"Lo what's up?"

"What's up, Cuz? What's hood?"

"Look, meet me at Belle Isle at midnight!"

"Midnight! A'ight, bet, I gotchu' you!"

I hung up the phone and headed straight to Tek's house. When I got there, he was sitting on the porch drinking a forty.

"What's up Homie??" I said as I approached the porch.

"What's hood, Dawggie?"

"Man that nigga put his hands on my momma!"

"WHO! Yo uncle?" He jumped to the edge of the chair.

"Naw man, her husband!"

"WHAT?"

"Yeah, Dawg, and I'm not having that shit at all. I already don't like the nigga as it is, so ima have to take care of that fool for real!"

"So what's up, whatchu' wanna do?", Tek said pulling out his shot gun from under his chair.

"Naw man, Ima take care of this one myself!"

"You sho', Homie? Cause you already know I'm yo guy!"

"Yea, I'm sho', but I do need another pistol. This nigga don' broke in my crib and took all my guns!"

Tek went into the house and moments later he came back with a plastic grey and black .380

"Oooh wee! Where you get this from?"

"You remember that Asian chick? Her father is the connect down in Japan!"

"Man that boy sweet as hell!", I said, holding this exclusive piece of work.

I already know it can do some damage, and I am gonna want to keep it instead of tossing it.

"Alright look, dig this!"

I told Tek about meeting with Lo at Belle Isle, and how I'm going to handle things.

"Dawg you sho' you don't need me?" Tek asked.

"Positive Homie, just let me work it out. Ima ditch the gun in the Detroit River and go back over to Canada for a lil while. Ima need you to keep check on my mom's for me too, a'ight?"

"Nough said Homie!" Tek replied.

We gave each other a hug and I walked to the car and took off. I popped in the Paper Trail CD and put it on "Ready for Whatever". I figured I'd ride through the city for one last time 'cause I know that after tonight's event, this could possibly be my last night for a while, if not forever.

I got to Belle Isle at about 11:30 and parked off to the right of the bridge with the view of Canada just across the Detroit River. Time was moving pretty fast so I just got out and sat on the hood contemplating; reviewing the past twenty eight years of my life, and thinking about how within the next hour my fate would be decided.

Sometimes in life you are going to make decisions where you are going to gamble or play it safe. Some people are lucky and some, not so lucky. I guess life sometimes takes its own route, and all you gotta do is just roll the dice. I once heard that the decisions you make today will create the path you walk tomorrow. Maybe I'll have a path to walk on instead of lay on.

Midnight is approaching and I stood up still looking across the waters, moments later....

"What's up, Cuz?" I heard Lo from behind me. I didn't bother turning around I kept my back towards him.

"What's up, Homie? I see you ain't waste no time in getting here. It ain't even midnight yet."

"Yeah... Well... When its business on the floor things gotta be done in a timely manner!"

"Business, what you mean by that? I asked. I heard his pistol cock back.

"Oh, it's like that huh?"

"I had no choice Dawg. You know how shit go." I went for my gun.

"Naw, Homeboy. Turn around." He ordered.

"I turned around and looked at him and the gun was shaking in his hand.

He looked to the left, then to the right, then I quickly drew my gun.

"So, you was going to try and do me in, huh? Nigga, I thought we were family?"

"Man, I'm sorry cuz; it was either you or me!"

"Who da hell is this?" I said looking at somebody coming from behind him. As he got closer I got a clearer view.

"Dawg, you got some nerve showing up here."

It was my mother's husband, Willie.

I immediately turned my pistol towards him instead of Lo, my gut was telling me to shoot him, and just as I was about to pull the trigger I see someone else coming from the woodworks.

"Oh, so ya'll need more than one to take me out, huh?'

They got closer and my heart began to beat fast and hard. My palms started to sweat as I was getting a clearer view of who it was.

"WHAT THE FUCK!" I yelled.

It was Tony and my uncle.

"What's up, Nephew? I got a surprise for you!"

Looking at Tony I almost lost it. I damn near lost my life tryna save his.

"Nigga I thought you were dead?" I shouted and everybody started laughing.

I kept switching my gun to who I thought I would kill first.

"You see nephew; I told you before that I know people, who know people. In this world we live in today, it's not about what you know, it's about who you know. See, Tony did owe my partners a few hundred dollars in jail, and the people he owed, owed me. Tony got out looking for a job, come to find out, you had a lil' shop downtown, What a coincidence. My partners told me you hired him, from there I saw it was a great opportunity to get a little closer to you, I gave Tony a lil' option that if he got closer to you that he would live. He's been keeping track on you every since. Oh yeah, I forgot, thanks for killing those kidnappers for me too. I really appreciate it. It's a shame what happened to yo' homeboy Hemmings. I had to serve you a little message letting you know I'm everywhere. Awl man, and that Bitch, Maria, OOOh Wee she can slob a nigga up real good. You shouldn't have fucked that up man I'm telling you. You went to that white girl, now you know better than that… Um um um!"

He shook his head with his eyes closed, and by that time I was so hot and heated, but I was out numbered. I should have just killed him in the club when I had the chance to.

"Just tell'em Smitty" said Willie.

"TELL ME WHAT?" I shouted back.

"Oh, so you think that we here because of that shit I told you when you were younger?"

"I'm listening"

He started laughing. "Ask yo' m-"

I saw everybody look behind me and I stepped back a lil tryna see who it was, and keeping my eye on them at the same time.

"Naw, it ain't going down like that, Homie!" It was Tek, Big Ray, and Doo Whop.

"Dawg, what you doing here?", I asked.

"I couldn't let you go out like this Dawg straight up. We don' been through too much Homie!"

Although I asked him not to come I was so happy to see them standing behind me, now it was a standoff. Me and my homies and my so called fam. I had my pistol pointing at Willie; Tek, Big Ray, and Doo Whop pointed at the others.

"So, this is how it is, huh?" I asked. "I thought ya'll was my family!"

"Yeah, well you fucked that up nephew, so like they say, it what it is."

He pulled out his pistol and cocked the four lb bar. I turned and looked at the fellas, pulled the hammer back, and nodded my head...

"Blayah!" "Poof!" "Poof!" "Poof!" "Pip!" "Pip!" "Pip!" "Blayah!" "Blayah!" "Doof!" "Doof!" "Doof!"

The sound of thunder sung through the air, as bullets were zipping past whistling through my ear drums saying this 'This is for you'

Smoke was everywhere and I was lying on the ground, I could barely move. I had been hit in the shoulder twice. I felt like every time I tried to move, the bullet would heat up.

"Tek!" I yelled

He didn't answer, and when I looked over at him he wasn't moving. I heard coughing

"Tek!" I yelled again

"I'm here, Homie!" He was coughin' again.

"You alright?'

"I got hit in the chest, but I had my vest on. It just knocked the wind outta me. I'm good though!"

I looked at Big Ray, and he was on his stomach motionless. Doo Whop was moving back and forth and it looked like he got shot in his hand; he had his hands between his legs trying to keep the blood from leaking.

I looked over at Tony and Lo and they weren't moving either. Tek went over to check on Big Ray.

"He's still breathing Dawg!" he yelled.

"SMITTY." I yelled as I looked up and seen him tryin' to run as he was hobbling toward the bridge holding his leg and shoulder. "Dammit!" I should have killed his ass when I had the opportunity. Fuck it! Let him run. I'll catch up to him sooner or later. He was looking for me and its time that the tables turn. I got up holding my right shoulder and slowly walked over to Tony and my cousin.

I looked at Lo and he had six bullets in his chest and stomach, and Tony had got hit in the eye. I looked at him up close and saw right through his skull. Blood was running out like this was movie scene.

"L.C!" Big Ray yelled, and I walked over to help Tek pick him up.

"Thank God we had on our vest, huh?" Big Ray said,

"Aye, we just in time!" Tek shouted.

"For what?" I asked

Tek looked towards the Belle Isle bridge, and I seen a big ass boat coming slowly across the water. It was that Asian chick from he bike races.

"Help me dump the bodies on it, she gon' ship their bodies to Japan and her father gone take care of the rest. Just make sure you don't eat any Chinese for a while. You never know what you'll be eating in that shit!", Tek said. We all tried to laugh but the bullet wounds wouldn't allow it.

We drug the bodies to the top of the bridge and once the flat bed passed under us, we through them over on to it.

"Tek!" I yelled.

"What's up Homie?"

"What made you come to where I was?"

"Listen, Dawg… Sometimes water can become thicker that blood!"

I guess he was right. Sometimes Blood Ain't Thicker Than Water. You will think that family will always come first and stand by your side for life, but in my case, it was my friends in the end that came through. I guess that's why they say, you should always watch the company you keep.

Sitting in the back seat, looking out the window as we rolled over the Belle Isle Bridge something didn't seem right. I couldn't quite get my finger on it. I back played everything that just happened and still couldn't figure it out. Then it hit me...

"WAIT!!" I shouted, and Tek stopped the truck.

"What's up, Dawg?" Tek answered.

"Where the fuck did my mom's husband go....?"

EPILOGUE

After spending a year in Canada, I figured that it was time to go back to Detroit; Bamby was excited to be back after spending all that time in Brandon, Manitoba. We even have a two month old son named, Junior. That's my little man too, and I love him to death. He really opened my eyes cause now I gotta buckle down with all this wild shit. I'm definitely not tryna go back to the joint, that's out the question.

I talked to my mom and she told me she hasn't seen her husband, Willie, since everything happened. That fool probably think I've been looking for him, I can't believe I let that nigga get away. When I do find him, and I will, its going to be a price to pay, and I don't mean with money.

It's Sunday and I know my grandfather has been looking for me every since we had that talk, wondering when I was going to show up. Ima give him a surprise today on his eighty second birthday. That crack's me up that he's in his eighties. Because he will let you know why he moves the way he does, "When yo get to be eighty, you'll see why you lay in bed all day" or "when you get to be my age, you can't sit for a long period of time, you'll see!" He's a character when it comes to his age, but he can still preach!

"Hey, how you doing, Brother Cook?", the usher said as I walked in the door.

"I'm blessed, you?"

"Oh, I'm highly favored. You holdin' on?"

"Yes, Sister Carlisle, I'm still holding on."

She asks me this every time she sees me!

She gave me a program and a fan and I went and sat in my usual seat, all the way in the back; I like to be able to see everything. My grandfather was preaching up a storm, and throughout him speaking he kept looking toward me. It was as if his words were directed to me. I gotta admit that after a while I began to feel this spirit come over me as it did when I was a youngster playing the drums.

I stood up.

"You betta preach!!" I said waiving my fan, as he was about to reach the climax of his sermon.

I happened to look out the window and seen a black Tahoe pulling up in the parking lot. It was nothing out of the ordinary, 'cause it's the same Black Tahoe that's been pulling up in the parking lot at 12:00 noon, since I was a child.

Like clockwork, Deacon Hunter looked at the clock, and made his way to the back door. He was walking across the street to the parking lot. He walked around to the back of the truck and opened the trunk. He usually leaves with two black duffle bags, but this time he came from behind and shook his head to whoever was in the driver seat.

He went back to the back of the truck, and again he came from behind and shook his head. I turned back around tryna to listen to what my grandfather was sayin' then I turned back to the outside. The driver and the passenger must have gotten out because both the doors were open, and as they came from the back of the truck I couldn't believe who I just saw…

"What the…!"

After all these years seeing this same transaction take place, I never saw who was in the truck. The truck pulled off and Deacon Hunter came back in the building and headed downstairs. I put my index finger in the air and followed right behind him. I walked down the steps and I heard noise sounding like he was pounding on the dinner tables.

"Deacon Hunter, what's up man?"

"He was walking back and forth with his hands on his head.

"Oh, Brother Leon, how you been?" He was breathing hard.

"Oh, I've been okay and now I'm even better!" I said with a slight grin on my face, as he looked confused.

"Deacon, I got a proposition for you. In this case you only have one option and that's to take it!"

He gave me his undivided attention.

"Now, I know, who you was just out_"

"Brother Leon, I--"

I cut him off just as he did me.

"Just listen! Now, I know who you were just dealing with outside, and all I want you to do is just get me closer to him, and if you do, and I know you will, you'll surely be blessed!"

He started pulling on his long beard thinking about what I had just said.

"Oh-okay, alright, I can do that for you Brother Leon. I'm suppose to meet up with him, Toni-"

"Hey grandson!", my grandfather said coming down the stairs.

"What's goin' on Granddad. Man, you was cutting up, up there today?"

"Oh yeah, God is good!"

"All the time!", I said back.

"And all the time!", he said.

"God is good!", I replied.

"I see you finally made it?"

"Yeah, it was time to come back home."

"Well come on here and get you something to eat, and fellowship for a while."

"Alright, sounds good. I'll be in there in a minute!"

He left to go sit down and I gave Deacon Hunter my number.

$$$

It's 1:43 in the morning and I just received a call from Deacon Hunter. He was supposed to meet up with his supplier at 2:00. I told him to change their drop spot, and to meet me at Rouge Park over on Plymouth and Burt Road, on the side of the pool.

I'm standing behind the building while Deacon Hunter was waiting alongside the pool for his supplier to arrive. I looked up and saw headlights and noticed that it was the Tahoe from earlier. Deacon Hunter turned and looked at me, and I nodded my head.

The driver opened his door first, and then the passenger. Seconds later the back door behind the driver door opened as well.

"Who the hell is this?" I thought to myself as three people got out the truck.

The person on the passenger side had two duffle bags in his hands, and they preceded walking inside the gate to meet with Deacon Hunter. The person that got out the back had a hat on and long hair like a woman that came down to the top of the shoulder. I had a good visual of all four people and could hear quite well.

"What are we doing here?" the driver asked.

"We had to change locations! Do you have the package now?" Deacon Hunter asked.

"Do you have the money?"

"Deacon threw a bag in between them.

I pulled out my pistol and cocked back the gun.

"Whoa! Who the hell is this?", the driver yelled as he saw me come from behind the building. All three guys drew their guns and as they got closer they began to see who I was. The person with the hat on kept his head down.

"Glad to see me, huh?", I asked walking towards them.

They looked at each other confused, tryna figure out how they both knew me.

"You know this nigga?", the Pookie look-alike asked the driver with his gun pointed.

"Yeah, I do! This is my wife's son!"

"Who the hell is that behind you?" I shouted. The man took off his hat and lifted his head up.

"What the FUCK!"

"Hi son…!"

It's my mom!

I looked her in the eyes, and I was hot, raging with fire. I didn't know what to say and then again I didn't want to say a word. I still had my pistol cocked, and for a split second I was about to pull the trigger and blow her head off, but I couldn't do it just yet. I need more answers, and I knew that this wasn't the time nor the place to get what I was looking for. I shook my head and looked at her baffled tryna' to put two and two together, and I kept coming up with four instead of twenty two.

What a coincidence that this is the same fool that I slapped that day when I seen Toya at the park. I know he haven't forgot about that and I am wondering what is going on in his head as well. How da fuck does he know my people for one, and does Toya know anything about this. I started backing up with the gun still pointed, and my mom took a step forward.

"Son, can we talk about this?"

She was tryna' plea, but I was not tryna' to hear it.

"What do you know about Smitty tryna' kill me, and why?"

I took a few more steps back.

"Please son, can we just talk about what is going--?"

"YOU TAKE ANOTHER STEP AND IMA BLOW YO MOTHER FUCKING HEAD OFF" I yelled, and she stopped dead in her tracks.

"Please L.C. There is something I never told you."

"SHUT THE FUCK UP!" I yelled again, and by that time I was twenty feet away. My gut was telling me that ties were about to become unknotted. It would be a matter of time before they all become loose. But I guess some things are better off done sooner rather then later.

"FUCK YOU!"

BLAKKA...

TO BE CONTINUED...

LAST WORDS...

Aye yo, what's up ya'll, what's hood? This ya boy, L.C, Man, this was a crazy story, huh? That's how it is sometimes, though. Your family can say they down for you, and got your back, or that you can trust them no matter what, through thick in thin, but when it's all said and done, Blood Really Ain't Always Thicker than Water!

You better believe it ain't over. I just had to end the story right there, cause it was just too much to tell, but if you want to hear some more about what happened in my life, holla at Rod on Facebook@ Sherradoneiltheauthor.

I hope ya'll picked up something from reading, cause I definitely did just by going through it, but hey... It is what it is.

I need ya'll to do me a favor though. Make sure ya'll check out Rod's next couple projects. "Cuffed". Now, that's a MUST READ!!

It's about a high school basketball superstar who's the number one player in the country. The night before he was suppose to head off to college he got caught up. Oh, and believe me, when I heard the story behind "Cuffed", it outright blew my mind. I saw him play when I was down too. He can really play his ass off. So, make sure ya'll check that out as well. If you thought this story was interesting, "You gon' love to hear this one!" "LIFE STARTS WHEN THE CHURCH ENDS" will be coming out soon too, so make sure you show some support.

It was good to vent with ya'll for real, but I gotta go now, my son needs his diapers changed. WAIT! Hold on my phone is going off.

"Whats up baby?"

"D-town, whats up Mon'?"

"What's good bro? Man thank ya'll fo-"

"They found out about the hit on Biggs."

"Yeah, and?" I stood up.

"There on they way to Detroit right now."

"WHAT?"

"And so are we"

Wholethang Publishing Co.
Sherrad O'Neil Glosson, CEO
P.O. Box 3383
Southfield, MI 48037

214

sherradglosson@gmail.com

www.ingramcontent.com/pod-product-compliance
Lightning Source LLC
Chambersburg PA
CBHW031329170626
46807CB00002B/620